DEATH OF A GUNFIGHTER

Lewis B. Patten

In his twenty years as marshal of Cottonwood Springs, Frank Patch had used hard means to tame the town . . . and now it was safe. But times had changed and the townsfolk wanted him and his guns out of the territory. When a harmless drunk tried to shoot him, Frank shot back and killed him. That set loose a chain of events that made the marshal the object of the town's hate . . . fanned into flaming rage by three killers. When Frank went after them, the citizens lined up against him and the marshal had to face impossible odds.

LEWIS B. PATTEN WESTERNS IN LARGE PRINT

Death Of A Gunfighter

The Ordeal Of Jason Ord

Posse From Poison Creek

Lewis B. Patten

DEATH OF A GUNFIGHTER

John Curley & Associates, Inc.
South Yarmouth, Ma.
1979

Library of Congress Cataloging in Publication Data

Patten, Lewis B
    Death of a gunfighter.

    Large print ed.
    1. Large type books. I. Title.
[PZ4.P316Dd 1979]   [PS3566.A79] 813'.5'4   78-21986
ISBN 0-89340-184-6

Published in Large Print by arrangement with Doubleday &
Company, Inc.

Distributed in the U.K. and Commonwealth by Magna Print
Books.

Printed in Great Britain

DEATH
OF A
GUNFIGHTER

Chapter 1

There was a certain comfort in routine but Frank Patch, marshal of Cottonwood Springs, Kansas, had always consciously avoided it. Routine set a man up for his enemies. It was dangerous for a lawman. It was much too dangerous for Patch. So he varied his movements deliberately from day to day. He seldom made his rounds of the town along the same route on any two successive days.

Tonight, his late evening tour took him down Elm, the town's main business street, toward the saloons below Texas Street. As always, he rode the big black horse and as always he made a fine target on the horse's back even though, from habit, he kept to the shadows as much as possible.

Times had changed. No one had taken a shot at Patch for years. But instinct

1

kept him careful, the same instinct that had kept him alive through all the turbulent, lawless years. The times had changed but Patch had not. In Patch the past was still alive.

He reined the black to a halt a block short of Texas Street, troubled by a vague and unaccustomed feeling of uneasiness. His eyes probed the shadows along both sides of the street.

Instinct told him there was danger waiting ahead of him. Reason might scoff and say it was impossible, but reason had never been able to quiet the animal instinct in him.

Tensely he rode ahead. Noise, plainly audible even a block away, poured from the open doors of the town's four saloons, the Goliad and the Alamo, the Drovers and the John Brown.

Frank Patch reined his horse suddenly off the street, across the walk and into the shadow of the Kansas Hotel, impelled by his uneasiness. He peered closely along the street, still seeing nothing threatening. He frowned.

2

He saw a man come out of the Goliad, a man who, at this distance, looked like a puncher from one of the ranches outside of town. The man staggered across the walk and fell when he tried to step down into the street. He got up with difficulty and staggered toward the hitch rail where half a dozen horses waited quietly.

Patch thought about going down there to see that the drunk got on the right horse. Otherwise he'd have a horse-stealing complaint on his hands later tonight, and he'd have to get Lou Trinidad, the county sheriff, to ride out tomorrow and recover the horse.

But Patch didn't move. He waited, still probing the darkness with his glance.

Maybe he was getting old, he thought. Maybe with age he was getting nerves. He was sure as hell jumpy tonight. The thing to do was to ride on and ignore his jumpy nerves. No danger was waiting for him. He was imagining things.

He touched the black's sides with his

3

heels, and the animal stepped out of the shadows and into the dim light cast in the street by the lamps inside the lobby of the hotel. He moved unhurriedly down Elm toward the drunk, who was still fumbling among the horses tethered in front of the Goliad.

Patch was squarely in front of the hotel when his ears caught a sound in the passageway between two buildings directly across the street. His arm had time to take in slightly on the horse's reins. His leg had time to tense, preparatory to dismounting from the horse. His right hand had time to poise itself over the holstered gun.

A voice yelled. "Patch! You son-of-a . . . , I . . ." The sentence was never finished. Flame spewed from the muzzle of a gun, and behind Patch the window of the hotel shattered explosively. Pieces of it cascaded to the walk.

Already tense, jumpy from his uneasiness, Patch's hand went with instinctive prompting to the smooth walnut grips of his holstered gun. Another shot ripped

4

from the gun across the street, and a third. The third bullet creased the rump of Patch's big black horse and made him jump.

Twenty years of living with danger took control of Patch. The gun slid smoothly from its holster the way it had many thousands of times before. Coming up, the hammer cocked from the pressure of his thumb. As the gun came into line, centering on the fading flash across the street, it fired, its recoil a familiar feel against his palm. Across the street the other gun fired yet another time, and once more Patch's gun roared with a better target this time, a muzzle flash that had not had time to fade.

He was off the horse by then, running toward the place from which the shots had come. He zigzagged as he ran, to throw off the hidden killer's aim.

But there was no need. A body lay on the sagging boardwalk, a body that didn't stir when Patch came near.

Gun in hand, he stopped. In the almost complete darkness here he failed to recognize the man immediately. He kicked the revolver, barely visible, out of the man's inert hand. Then he knelt, holstering his gun.

The body lay face down. Patch turned it over. A reek of whiskey lifted, but no breathing stirred the chest. The man was dead.

Behind him, Patch heard a shout, followed by the murmuring of voices from the hotel veranda across the street. He turned his head and yelled, "Bring a lantern over here!"

But he didn't need the light now to recognize the man. He knew it was Luke Mills.

He got slowly to his feet. Why? In God's name, why had Luke shot at him? Why had Luke wanted him dead? It didn't make any sense.

A man approached from the hotel, a lantern in his hand. He was followed by others, some not completely dressed. A voice said unbelievingly, "It's Luke! For God's sake, it's old Luke Mills!"

Another voice asked, "What

6

happened, Marshal? What happened here?"

It was the voice of Andrew Oxley, who published the town's weekly newspaper.

Patch looked at him. "He just opened up on me as I rode past the hotel. Do you have any idea why he'd do a stupid thing like that?"

Oxley knelt at Mill's side. He got up immediately. "He'd been drinking. He must have been so drunk he didn't know what he was doing. Good Lord, did you have to kill him, Frank?"

Patch stared. "What do you mean, did I have to kill him? It's dark out here. He was in that passageway and he ambushed me. He shot at me four times."

Oxley did not reply. He turned his head. "Somebody had better get the undertaker. And somebody will have to tell his wife."

A voice in the crowd said, "Maybe the minister – maybe Mr. Rork would tell her . . ."

Oxley said, "All right. Go ask him to."

Patch drew his revolver and began automatically to punch the empties out. Oxley stared at him. Patch reloaded the gun from his cartridge belt before replacing it. He looked up and met Oxley's disapproving glance. The mayor, Chester Sayre, had appeared from somewhere and now stood at Oxley's side.

Irritation stirred in Patch. He said, "Damn it, don't look at me like that. I didn't know it was Luke in the passage-way, and I sure as hell didn't know that he was drunk."

Sayre said evenly, "I've seen you disarm a drunk that was shooting at you and yelling threats."

Patch said, "That was twenty years ago. I knew he was drunk and who he was. This was different."

"Was it, Frank?"

Frank grunted disgustedly and walked back across the street to his horse. Blood was dribbling down the horse's leg from the wound on his rump.

He stroked the horse's neck a few

moments to quiet him. His face was angry, but it was puzzled too.

A man of medium height, Frank Patch always seemed taller than he really was. People who had met him only once would say of him that he was over six feet tall. It was the way they remembered him. But he wasn't. He was only five feet nine, a thickset man with broad, powerful shoulders, a deep, strong chest, a bit of a paunch these days, slim hips and short, sturdy legs.

His arms were long for the rest of him, and he wore his gun low against his thigh so that he did not have to raise his hand very much to reach its grip.

Tight woolen trousers and Texas high-heeled boots. Gunbelt sagging, supporting the holstered .45. A fresh white cotton shirt and a frayed vest to which was pinned his silver marshal's star.

His hair was like the mane of a lion, graying these days, long on his thick neck and around his ears. He wore a black, high-crowned Stetson hat that he seldom took off his head. He was all male, an old bull, a scarred stallion, a lean old dog-wolf. He was the law here and he had been the law for more than twenty years.

Nothing like this had ever happened to him before. It was like a dream he'd sometimes had when he'd first become marshal. In the dream he killed a lawbreaker only to discover when he looked closely that it was a friend.

He swung to the horse's back. Down the street, men were now pouring from the saloons, hurrying curiously up the street to see what the commotion was about. Patch rode past them, heading for the lower end of Elm, heading for the railroad tracks and the loading pens, continuing his rounds.

He suddenly wanted to be alone. He didn't want anybody else asking him if he'd had to kill Luke Mills.

He'd killed Luke and that was that. He'd acted in the defense of his life. He hadn't known it was Luke, and he hadn't known Luke was drunk.

He couldn't begin to understand why Luke Mills had tried to kill him anyway. There could be only one possible explanation.

The townspeople had been trying to make him quit his job for almost a year. They grumbled that he was out of his place in time. They said he gave newcomers and visitors a bad impression and made them think that Cottonwood Springs was so lawless a gunfighter was needed to keep the peace.

They wanted uniformed policemen, they said, as other towns already had. They wanted a trolley car running up and down Elm Street. They wanted progress and growth, and he stood in the way. They wanted him to quit.

So far he had steadfastly refused. Grimly now he thought that refusing was his right. They'd made a contract with him when he took the marshal's job more than twenty years ago. They'd told him he could have the job for as long as he wanted it, as inducement to get him to take on the task of pacifying the wild and

11

lawless town. Certainly the pay hadn't been enough to make him risk his life half a hundred times the first year he was on the job.

There had been grumbling when he refused to quit. That was inevitable, he supposed. There had even been talk that they'd make him quit whether he wanted to or not. How they proposed to make him do anything he didn't want to do, no one had said.

Luke must have been trying to rid the town of him. He must have been drunk enough to take seriously their talk of progress being dependent on ridding themselves of the marshal. He must have thought he could make himself important by killing Patch.

It was unbelievable but it was the only explanation that made any sense at all. Patch suddenly felt as if he had been used. He felt as if he had been forced into a false position from which it was impossible for him to escape.

Chapter 2

Young Dan Joslyn was cold when he awoke. The covers were pulled tight around his body and up beneath his chin. The air coming in the open window was cool but not that cool. Dan was cold because he was scared. And he had reason to be scared. He figured the whole town did. Because this was the day they were going to try to get rid of Patch.

Two weeks had passed since Patch had shot Luke Mills in front of the Kansas Hotel, two weeks of heated discussion and sour grumbling while determination firmed in the minds of the townspeople. But now the day was here.

Dan lay there still for a long time, staring at the window curtains moving with the light morning breeze, staring at the dazzling sunlight streaming in, at the brilliant yellow leaves on the gnarled old

13

cottonwood just outside the second-story window of his back room at Ma Jorgensen's boardinghouse. There was a feel in the air today, a smell, a chill, a thing that stirred the instincts of animals and men. Winter was on its way.

He swung his feet over the edge of the bed and put them, bare, onto the floor. He threw the covers off and stood up, a tall, stringy, skinny-shanked boy of fifteen who would be sixteen next week. There was a light, fuzzy stubble on his face that he shaved off once a week. His yellow hair was uncut and now mussed from sleep. He walked to the window and stared down into the back yard where clothes were already on the line. He turned away hurriedly, guiltily. There were chores to be done, and he'd overslept. It must be almost six.

He dressed hastily, in faded jeans and cotton shirt, then sat down and pulled on the boots Patch had given him two days ago in anticipation of his sixteenth birthday the middle of next week. He frowned as he did so, troubled by conflicting beliefs and loyalties. Frank Patch was his friend. But the town said Patch was a killer and dangerous now. They were going to get rid of him.

Frank Patch had been marshal of Cottonwood Springs as long as Dan could remember and before. Like the town, he'd been here before Dan was born. He'd been hired back in '68 when trail herds from Texas were hitting the Kansas rail towns three or four times a week.

Patch had been hired to protect the town from the drovers and from the scum and riffraff they attracted after a bunch of drunken drovers "treed" the town and kept it "treed" for a day and night while they shot up buildings and signs, broke into stores, terrified the town's respectable citizens and drove its womenfolk underneath their beds.

Patch had changed things almost immediately, if a week can be called immediately. He killed five men and wounded several more. In the end, he drew a line down the middle of one of the cross streets which he had renamed Texas Street. He said that henceforth drovers, saloons and bawdy houses and their occupants were to stay below the line. Even today there wasn't a saloon this side of Texas Street.

Dan hurried down the narrow stairs, went into the hot kitchen where breakfast was cooking on the huge, cast-iron range and on beyond to the back porch and outside. He crossed the yard to the woodshed, loaded his arms with wood and hurried back. Only when the woodbox beside the stove was full again did he stop to wash up at the pump.

After that, he got two buckets on the back porch and began to refill the huge, copper clothes-boiler on the stove.

By this time, the dining room was beginning to fill with boarders, and he helped Ma and her daughter Hilda by filling coffee cups and carrying in huge platters of food. When the boarders had finished eating and the dining room had turned hazy-blue with pipe and cigar smoke, he filled a plate for himself and went out on the back steps to eat.

Hilda came out and sat down beside him. They had quarreled yesterday about Patch. Now she seemed to want to make up, but Dan wasn't ready yet.

Hilda asked timidly, "You still mad at me?"

He kept his eyes on his plate. "You just don't know him, that's all. He ain't like they say he is. He ain't changed a bit. He's just like he always was."

Hilda didn't answer him. She was almost as tall as he, slender but strong-boned like her mother. Her hair, braided and coiled atop her head, was yellow as straw and fine as silk. Her eyes were blue; her skin, fair. There was a little bridge of pale freckles across her nose. She made a concession for the sake of peace. "You know a lot more about him than I do, Dan. I guess you're right."

"Sure I'm right." His tone was a grumble, but there was less hostility in him than there had been before. He stared down at the boots. They were the finest calfskin a man could buy, Patch

17

had said when he gave them to him. Dan had intended to put them away and save them for good, but Frank Patch told him, "You wear them, boy. That's the way to enjoy a thing. Use it. What good'll them boots do you if you put 'em in a closet and let your feet get too big for 'em?"

He could almost hear Patch's calm, deep voice talking to him. He could almost see the man's face when he looked down at the boots. He liked Frank Patch. He wanted to be like the marshal when he was fully grown. But he was a little afraid of Frank Patch, too. Everyone was afraid of Patch.

Maybe it was the legend that had grown up around his name. Maybe it was the stories about him that had been told and retold until nobody knew how much of each story was truth and how much fantasy. Maybe it was the commanding presence he made sitting up on his great black horse, his old Colt Peacemaker resting lightly against his thigh. Maybe it was the sharp, authoritative look in his blue eyes or the long, shining mustache that swept away so grandly on both sides of his mouth. Or maybe it was just that Patch was so everlastingly sure of himself that no one else dared to doubt him.

Hilda's voice was still timid when she spoke again. "What's going to happen, Dan? What if he keeps on refusing to quit even when everybody goes down there together to tell him he's got to quit?"

Dan didn't know. That was what had been worrying him. It was like wondering what would happen when an irresistible force met an immovable object. He had heard talk lately, some of it pretty reckless talk. He'd heard them saying that if Patch wouldn't quit, they'd use force. Just the thought of what might happen to Patch made Dan's stomach churn.

Hilda asked, "Why is it suddenly so important, anyway? Is it because of him killing Luke Mills two weeks ago?"

Dan realized that Hilda was trying to

make him talk, trying to draw him out so that he'd forget their argument. Last night she'd said Patch hadn't had to kill Luke Mills, who was drunk when he'd challenged the marshal on the street. Dan had argued with her and defended Patch, but he'd known all the time that what she said might be true. Patch might have handled it without killing Luke. He'd disarmed drunks before without killing them. Or at least that's what people said. Anyway, it wasn't just the killing of Luke two weeks ago. That had only brought things to a head.

He said, "Everyone says Patch belongs in the past. They say we need a regular police force now like they have in other towns."

They were saying other things, too, things Dan couldn't bring himself to repeat or even to think about. They were saying Patch was gun-crazy and dangerous. They were saying he ought to be put away for good.

Dan got up suddenly and carried his plate and cup into the kitchen. Hilda followed, staring at his back, puzzled.

He put down his plate and cup, then turned and hurried outside to the woodshed. He picked up the ax and went to work. He was strong and he had split a lot of wood. There was a competent economy of movement about the way he worked. He began to sweat.

But work didn't stop his thoughts the way he had hoped it would. Nor did it erase the worried frown his forehead wore. His eyes stayed just a little scared.

This morning Frank Patch awoke at five just as he always did. He dressed, and washed, and shaved in cold water, and then unlocked the door of his room at the hotel and descended the stairs to the lobby.

Coming down the stairs, he always swept the tile-floored lobby with a careful glance, noting each occupant. This morning there was only Lonnie Wegener, the clerk, dozing with his chair tilted back against the wall behind the desk.

Walking lightly toward the door

leading to the street, Patch frowned. There was something wrong in the way he felt today. It was as though he knew something was going to happen, as though he was unconsciously waiting and watching for it.

He was too old a hand to dismiss such a feeling as being of no consequence. A dozen times or more, hunches had saved his life.

He stepped out onto the hotel veranda almost warily, glancing immediately up and down the street.

The sun had not yet flooded Elm Street. It was just now touching the high tops of the giant old cottonwoods that lined the residential streets beyond. The air was fresh and cool, and had that fragrance which fall mornings sometimes possessed when dew lay heavy on the prairie grass beyond the town limits. Patch took a long, deep breath, smelling an indefinable hint of winter in the air.

From the hotel veranda, he stared down Elm toward the lower end of town, toward the railroad tracks and the station and the loading pens beyond, which were not used much these days and had largely fallen into disrepair. A block below the hotel, Texas Street crossed Elm. Sam Houston Street was next. Goodnight Street was the last one to cross short of the station and the railroad tracks.

Elm ran north and south. Paralleling it to the east was Maple, and beyond that, Oak. These were the two main residential streets. West of Elm were a couple of other streets where the town's poorer residents lived. They were called A Street and B Street for lack of more imaginative names.

Cottonwood Creek meandered along between A and B, from the upper end of town to the lower, creating a brushy bottomland that drew kids as a magnet draws iron filings. Nights, it drew the town's young people when they wanted to be alone. A dozen times in the last twenty years it had drawn a fugitive, hoping to use its cover to escape from Patch.

There was a cottonwood tree in the creek bottom not far from the railroad station that had been used as a scaffold in the early days. The limb from which they'd hanged the prisoners still was there, and sometimes Patch would ride down that way when making his rounds. He would sit on his horse and look up at it and remember, and sometimes he'd see the faces of those who had died there in his mind. Lately, he had been coming here every day.

A lot of faces paraded through Patch's mind at one time or another, the faces of men dead by his own hand over the years. He felt no real regret over killing them. There had been justification in every case.

Justification in every case. He frowned, his mind closing against the memory of Luke Mills. He'd already asked himself a hundred times if killing Luke had been a necessity, and yet what else could he have done?

He stepped down off the veranda and walked along the boardwalk toward his

24

office in the jail.

The building was constructed of dun-colored sandstone quarried from the bluff a mile east of town. It was one of the oldest buildings in Cottonwood Springs, having been one of the town's first necessities. It sat back from the street and was fenced, and it had a little plot of uncut grass in front. Lodgepole-pine timbers supported the roof, extending out eight feet beyond the sandstone walls in front to form a kind of gallery or porch. Patch had a couple of benches there and a single, creaking rocking chair, though he never used the rocker himself.

Behind the jail there was a small stable, big enough for a single horse. This was where Frank Patch kept the black. There was a pump nearby and there was a lean-to shed adjoining, where he kept the horse's hay. Grain he stored inside the jail in a tight wooden barrel to keep it safe from mice.

He rounded the jail, walking lightly in the high weeds, still troubled by a strange uneasiness, more watchful even than usual. He entered the stable, and the black turned his head to nicker softly at him.

Patch crossed to the horse and stroked his neck. He bridled the animal, flung up saddle blanket and saddle, then cinched the saddle down. He led the horse outside and mounted effortlessly.

Although he had tried to avoid routine, he realized suddenly that his whole life had been a routine of sorts. The black was fifteen years old. The jail was older, and he himself was older still. Yet none of the three had changed. Nor would they change, in spite of what the town's prominent citizens wanted nowadays.

He reined the horse around and rode through the tiny, grassy yard to the street. He headed straight down Elm toward the railroad tracks and the loading pens. He passed the John Brown Saloon, which was last in line and stood on the corner of Sam Houston and Elm streets.

The next block held a number of dilapidated frame residences, some abandoned, some with weed-filled yards, some without. Here were the town's brothels, three in all. There were two girls in one, a single girl in each of the other two. They were permitted to remain, although regularly two or three times a year the women of the church tried to have them driven out of town. Lately the mayor and the town council, reacting to this pressure, had been blaming Patch for their inability to get rid of the girls. They told their wives that Patch simply refused to run the girls out.

Patch reached the railroad station, halted his horse while he briefly scanned the premises, then rode on down the tracks toward the bed of Cottonwood creek. He went straight to the hanging tree and stopped.

The ground was littered with yellow leaves that the sun was just now touching with its warmth. The tree rustled faintly in the early morning breeze.

Patch stared up at the limb where so

many men had lost their lives. He stared up, and his eyes narrowed with remembering. A lot of time had passed. A lot of his life was here in this town, in Cottonwood Springs. Now they were trying to get rid of him, but he was damned if he was going to let them get away with it.

There wasn't much that scared Frank Patch. No tangible thing, nothing physical could make him feel afraid. But the thought of not being marshal of Cottonwood Springs could, and did. That thought turned him cold.

What would he do, he wondered. Where could he go? He'd be nothing and he might as well be dead.

That thing two weeks ago . . . Hell, it hadn't been his fault and they were wrong to blame him for it. He hadn't known Luke Mills was drunk. What he had known was that Mills called a challenge to him, and fired first. What he had done had been dictated by instinct and reflex, and he couldn't have stopped himself if he'd tried.

A challenge, right here on Elm Street,

right in front of the hotel, and yet they kept saying the past was gone, that they didn't need him any more. He scowled savagely but there was something troubled and confused in his eyes as they stared up at the towering cottonwood.

Chapter 3

Claire Quintana had a room at the Kansas Hotel, down the hall from the marshal's room. She was the only one connected with the part of town below Texas Street who was allowed this side of it. It was a concession the marshal had made to her. No one would have protested anyway because the deadline at Texas Street was no longer necessary, but it was still enforced.

Claire owned the Goliad. She was Patch's girl. Everyone in town knew it, and Claire liked it that way. She didn't have to be fighting off advances from every man in town. She didn't have every whiskey drummer that hit the Goliad slobbering over her. They called her "Miss Claire," or "Missus Quintana," and they were respectful even when Frank Patch wasn't there.

30

Claire was tall for a woman, five feet seven in bare feet. She was thirty, some years younger than Patch, but that was all right, too. She was a full-bodied woman – voluptuous was the word for her, she supposed, but again she liked it that way. And so, apparently, did Patch.

Like everyone else in town, Claire was afraid of Patch but she didn't quite know why. He had never struck her in the five years she had been here in Cottonwood Springs, in the five years she had been his girl. He had never been angry with her. He had never, by word or glance, threatened her or offered her any kind of harm.

But to Claire, Frank Patch was a tiger that has been tamed, a tiger that purrs like a house cat when its fur is being stroked, one that licks the hand with a wet pink tongue, but a tiger all the same with a tiger's fierceness and savagery slumbering somewhere deep inside.

She knew there was trouble coming for Frank. She knew the town intended to be rid of him, one way or another, no matter what they had to do. She also knew Patch would not go willingly because he knew what enforced retirement would do to him.

Now, he was a personage, a presence, a part of the town itself. He had grown with it, defended it, patrolled it, watched over it. He knew every boy in town by his first name. He knew what those boys were interested in and what they did with their time.

He knew the adults as well. He knew which of the respectable ones visited the brothels below Sam Houston Street. He knew which of the wives sometimes slipped out of the Kansas Hotel by a rear door late at night.

What would he be, without authority, without a job, without a place in the community? Claire walked to the window of her room and stared moodily down into the street.

It was only a little after five, but she was tired. She hadn't slept at all last night. She'd closed the Goliad at midnight and had come home to the hotel where she'd paced the floor until two. She had finally gone to bed and tried vainly to go to sleep. At last, at five, she had gotten out of bed and begun to pace the floor again.

Why should she worry so about Frank Patch? She wasn't in love with him. She was actually afraid of him even when she was in his arms. He was almost old enough to be her father.

She saw him come out onto the hotel veranda and look up and down the street. She saw the solidity of the man, the strength, the power and the fearlessness. She saw the almost animal way he walked, like some ancient predator looking for his morning kill.

She watched him walk down Elm toward his office in the jail. She saw him disappear, and reappear later mounted on his tall, gleaming black. He rode down Elm toward the railroad station and disappeared in the direction of Cottonwood Creek.

Making his rounds, she thought with a wry, small smile. Just as he has for twenty

33

years. Making his rounds even though there hadn't been a trail hand or a Texas trail herd in town for eighteen years. She turned away from the window.

She'd heard it said in the Goliad that he was out of date, and why the hell didn't the mayor and the town council fire him? Even those who asked the question knew the answer to it. Patch wouldn't quit. He had refused every time he'd been asked and so far no one had had the temerity to force his retirement.

Wearily, Claire began to dress. She'd help Frank today if she had the opportunity. The trouble was, she didn't know what she could do.

Chester Sayre was almost as much a permanent fixture in Cottonwood Springs as Frank Patch was. He had been mayor for sixteen years and had been here at the time of the first trail drives. He'd been a cattle buyer then. He'd made a sizable stake in two years buying Texas cattle and shipping them east by rail, and then had started a dry goods store.

He knew, as well as anyone, that Frank Patch was an anachronism. There would be no noticeable progress in Cottonwood Springs until Patch was gone. People typed a town just like they typed the people they met. They typed Cottonwood Springs the minute they saw Frank Patch making his rounds on that damn big black horse. They didn't want to start a business and settle in a town that needed a gunfighter to keep it orderly.

Sayre knew that Frank Patch had to go. It was even more urgent since the killing of Luke Mills two weeks ago. What he didn't know was how to get rid of Patch. He'd tried firing the man, but Patch had just smiled frostily and mentioned a certain lady with whom Sayre had been involved a couple of years ago. It was outrageous and it was blackmail, but it worked.

Patch had spent twenty years as marshal in the community and he knew things about its citizens they'd rather nobody knew. He knew things about a few of its prominent citizens that would ruin them if he told.

Yet in spite of his frustration, Sayre found it hard to blame Patch for making use of the only weapon that was left to him. Patch had his back to the wall. He was fighting for his life.

Sayre had always liked a brisk walk early in the day. In summer, he arose at five, washed and dressed and went out for his walk. Even in winter he took his early morning walk, though the hour grew later as winter came on, corresponding loosely to the rising of the sun.

He came into Elm above the hotel in time to see Patch disappear behind the jail, and he knew the marshal was going after his big black horse so that he could make his morning rounds.

Sayre smiled faintly as he walked down the street. He knew where Patch would go today. He'd been going down to that cottonwood in the creek every morning for the last two weeks, ever since he had killed Luke Mills on the street. The mayor's smile twisted wryly, but with reluctant sympathy. Every morning for two weeks, like a ritual, an atonement for what had happened two weeks ago right here in front of the hotel.

Andrew Oxley was standing in front of the newspaper office. "Good morning, Andrew. I'm going to try and catch Patch down by the old cottonwood and talk to him. Want to come along?" Sayre asked.

Oxley nodded, though without enthusiasm. He fell into step beside Sayre, and the two walked toward Texas Street. They turned the corner and headed for the creek. The sun came up, touching the tops of the tall cottonwoods, making their yellow leaves flame like torches, lighting the shadows underneath.

Cottonwood Creek flowed sluggishly at this time of year, except occasionally when a cloudburst swelled its flow. Sayre and Oxley walked thoughtfully and silently along the lip of the ravine toward the old cottonwood at the lower end of town.

Sayre saw the black and Patch, beside the gnarled, thick trunk of the ancient cottonwood as he and Oxley came through the brush. Patch heard them and whirled, his hand going to his gun.

It was a melodramatic gesture, from out of the long dead past, but neither Sayre nor Oxley smiled. Sayre said, "Morning, Frank."

Patch nodded briefly. He stared down from the horse's back at the two with neutrality. And suddenly it came to Sayre that Patch had no friends. He had no close friends at all, among adults at least. And that seemed strange for a man who had been here twenty years.

Sayre packed his pipe, lighted it and puffed thoughtfully. Oxley seemed strangely ill at ease. At last Sayre said pleadingly, "Give it up, Frank. Give it up and save everybody a lot of grief. The whole town wants you to."

Patch raised a hand and tugged gently at his mustache, something he never did unless he was upset. His eyes were cold and hard. "Because of Luke Mills? Hell, you know he didn't give me any choice. Besides, I remember things that were said twenty years ago, even if you don't. This was a scared town when they hired me. They made promises. I was to hold this job as long as I wanted it."

"Things change, Frank. This isn't the town it used to be."

"Maybe not. But look at what happened two weeks ago. If I hadn't been here, Luke might have challenged somebody else. He might have killed them, too. And anyway, it's not just that. This could turn into a wild town again if I took off my badge."

"The trail hands have stopped coming, Frank. Why would it get wild?"

"People don't change much."

Oxley interrupted, "There's no use talking to him Ches. He isn't going to quit."

"Then we'll have to get rid of him some other way."

Patch studied the two with smoldering eyes. "How else? How?"

Sayre said lamely, "We could stop

paying you."

Patch smiled humorlessly. "That won't do it, Ches, and you damn well know it won't. I've got a little put away and it don't take me much to live."

"We could get a court order and get the county sheriff to serve it on you."

"Lou Trinidad? He'd serve the paper but he wouldn't do anything else. He wouldn't enforce it. Not Lou."

Sayre stared at him, exasperated. He said angrily, "Don't push us, Patch. I was here twenty years ago myself, and maybe there's some of the old times left in me just like there is in you. We'll find a way."

Sayre glowered silently. Patch stared steadily down from the back of his big black horse, and Sayre suddenly felt like a little boy.

Patch shifted his cold glance to Oxley, standing beside Sayre. He said harshly, "You'd better keep out of this, Mr. Oxley, if you know what's good for you. You understand?"

Oxley did not reply, but his face lost

color and his mouth grew firm. He turned and stalked away, and Sayre followed him.

When they were out of Patch's hearing, Sayre asked, "Now what the hell did he mean by that?"

Oxley's voice was curt. "How the hell should I know, Ches? How should I know what Patch means by anything?"

Chapter 4

Mary Mills awoke that morning with the same feeling of loss with which she had awakened every morning for the last two weeks. She turned her head automatically to look at Luke, but her gaze encountered only emptiness. Luke was dead. The marshal had shot him in front of the Kansas Hotel two weeks ago.

Frank Patch may have shot Luke, but her own sharp tongue had forced Luke to try shooting Patch. She always came back to that.

She got up suddenly, impatient with the way her thoughts slipped into the same old rut. She dressed quickly, unbraided and combed her hair and put it up. She made the bed quickly. Going out into the kitchen, she shook down the ashes and built a fire in the stove. Only

42

when she had the coffee pot on did she sit down.

She wished she could stop her thoughts, wished she could make her mind a blank. She could not, because she knew why Luke had challenged Patch. He'd done it to prove to her and to everyone that he could do something no one else dared to do.

Luke had never amounted to very much. He hadn't been a businessman. He had worked for others, at whatever jobs he could find. He had worked for the mayor for half a dozen years, but Chester Sayre had finally let him go because Luke had been drunk once too often on the job.

Now she asked herself if perhaps she hadn't been the reason Luke drank so much and guiltily admitted that at least part of the responsibility had been hers. All through their married life, whenever she had gotten scared, or worried, or unhappy, she had taken it out on Luke by lashing him with her tongue, until it had become a habit, until she would do it

43

even when there had been no immediate reason for it.

It wasn't easy admitting this to herself. She had spent the last two weeks trying to avoid admitting this, but she couldn't avoid it any more.

She asked herself another question she had never asked before. Had she loved Luke or had she married him because no one else had asked her and because she knew if she didn't marry him, she would never marry anyone? She didn't like the answer to that question any more than she'd liked the answer to the other one.

Still, she told herself, she had tried to be a good wife to Luke. She had made a good home for him. She had worked as hard or harder than he had. But she hadn't made him happy. She'd made him miserable. They hadn't had children, and she'd blamed him openly for that. She'd blamed him because there had never been enough money to buy the things other people had, like dresses bought in the dry goods store ready-made, or trips to Kansas City, or even a horse and buggy of their own.

Drinking had been Luke's way of escaping her. It had made him feel less like a failure, at least until the effects wore off. But his drinking had also killed him, or helped to kill him. Under the influence of alcohol he'd thought he could do what no one else in town could do. He'd thought he could get rid of Patch.

Having accepted the responsibility for what had happened to Luke, Mary Mills now wondered how she was going to be able to live with her guilt. How was she going to forget that she had tongue-lashed him into trying to prove he was not as worthless as she had said he was?

Angrily she thought that Patch hadn't had to shoot Luke even if Luke had fired first. Several of the people who had seen the shooting had told her that. Patch had disarmed more dangerous men than Luke in the past. She remembered one story she'd heard about the marshal's walking calmly into the middle of the street to face a fusillade by a drunken trail hand who had challenged him and had sworn to rid the town of him. Patch hadn't even bothered to draw his gun but had knocked the man senseless with his fist, disarmed him and hauled him off to jail.

Others had told her Patch had done the only thing he could with her husband. Patch hadn't known Luke was drunk. It had been dark, and chances were he hadn't even recognized Luke until after he'd drawn and fired his gun. A gunfighter has reflexes, they told her. His hands sometimes work instinctively, independently of his brain.

She didn't know what to believe. She did know Luke was gone. All she had left was this feeling of guilt and the memory of standing in the light drizzle at the funeral, dressed in black, black-veiled and weeping. Patch had stood on the other side of the grave, his big black hat in his hands, wearing the black suit he wore at funerals. He had avoided looking at her. He had not approached her to say he was sorry for what he had done.

Luke was gone, and none of the cruel things she had said to him could now be taken back. That much was Frank Patch's fault.

If there was only something she could do that would ease this unbearable feeling of guilt! But there was not. It was too late.

Right now she had to eat. She had to eat if she were going to live. She had lost fifteen pounds in the past two weeks simply because she hadn't cared enough to prepare her meals. If it hadn't been for the neighbors bringing things in for her, she would have lost more weight than that.

She also had to try forgetting how Luke had died. She had to try to forget that she was responsible, or at least that she shared the responsibility with Patch.

She sliced some salt pork and put it on to fry. She went out to the back porch and got a couple of eggs she had gathered fresh in the henhouse yesterday. One of the neighbors had brought her a loaf of bread yesterday, and she cut two slices of it.

The coffee began to boil, filling the room with its fragrance. Mary cooked her eggs and put them on a plate with the salt pork, which was fried crisp by then. She sat down to eat. She stared at the empty place across from her.

And suddenly, seemingly out of nowhere, a smoldering hatred was born in her. She hated the marshal for emptying that place. She might have nagged and belittled Luke, but it was the marshal who had shot him down.

She finished eating, anger growing with the hatred in her heart. Someone ought to do something about Frank Patch. Someone ought to stop him from doing to anyone else what he had done to Luke. There ought to be ways of enforcing the law without shooting people in the street.

The sun was well up in the sky when Dan Joslyn left Ma Jorgensen's boarding-

48

house and headed toward the marshal's office on Texas Street and Elm, although it was not yet seven o'clock. He was sweating and out of breath, but the wood chopping had done for him what hard work always did. It had helped to clear his thoughts. It had helped him make up his mind.

One thing now stood out above all other things in his thoughts. Frank Patch was his friend. Patch had been good to him; in some ways Patch had been like the father he had never had. Patch had taught him what it is to be a man. Patch had given him these boots, and Dan knew what they'd cost at Sayre's Dry Goods Store. Patch had talked with him when he'd desperately needed someone to talk things over with.

But long ago Patch had done far more than that. When Dan's aunt had died six years before, there had been nobody to take care of the boy, and they were getting ready to send him off to Kansas City to the orphanage. Then Patch stepped in.

Patch talked to Ma Jorgensen and arranged for her to keep Dan in return for his doing chores. Patch vouched for him, made himself responsible for Dan's proper upbringing, and Dan didn't have to go away.

It was getting close to seven when Dan rounded the corner of Elm and Texas streets. Patch's big black horse was tied to the hitch rail in front of the sandstone jail. Dan stopped and briefly petted the horse's neck. The black nuzzled him, but Dan didn't have anything for him today. He left the horse, went through the gate, and walked along the dirt path to the door.

The marshal was sitting at his cluttered, roll-top desk. He had a stubby pipe between his teeth and the office smelled fragrantly of tobacco smoke.

Patch turned his head and glanced at Dan. "Well. You're out early today. Chores all done?"

Dan said, "Mostly done. I had to talk to you."

"Talk away. How's the boots? They fit

50

all right?"

"They fit just fine. And I like them fine." Now that he was here, he didn't quite know what to say. What he had intended to tell the marshal seemed silly now – the little things he'd overheard at the boardinghouse, bragging threats that were probably no more than that.

Patch was watching him. "You in trouble or something, boy?"

Dan shook his head. "It ain't anything like that. It's you."

"Me?"

Dan didn't know why but the room suddenly seemed colder than it had before.

"I don't mean that, exactly, Mr. Patch. It ain't nothing you've done. It's just that I sometimes hear things down at the boardinghouse. I ain't one to go carryin' stories an' you know that's so, but I just got to thinking maybe you ought to know what they're sayin' about you down at the boardinghouse."

"What are they saying, Dan?" Patch's voice was smooth, soft, like velvet, and it

51

frightened the boy.

But he was here. He swallowed and said, "A whole bunch of the townspeople are coming down here today. They're going to tell you you've got to quit."

"And if I won't?"

Dan's face was red, and he was sweating heavily. He said, "It's likely only big-mouthed talk. You know how people are. But a couple of 'em said if you won't quit peaceable like there's other ways to get rid of you."

Patch started to ask him which one had said that, then changed his mind. Dan was relieved when he did. It was one thing to tell things that had been said. It was another to tell who said them. That was snitching.

Patch sat still for a long time, not saying anything, puffing deliberately on his pipe. Out in the street Swenson's milk delivery wagon clattered past. Patch stared out the open door at it, and a wry smile touched his mouth. He said, "Milk comes in bottles now. That's progress, I guess. Time'll come, though, when kids won't even know milk comes from the udder of a cow."

Dan said, "Plenty of people still have cows." It seemed a funny thing to be talking about right now.

The marshal glanced away from the open door and looked at Dan. His eyes gleamed strangely now; they had an intensity Dan had never seen in them before. Patch didn't seem to see Dan at all, seemed in fact to be looking through him the way you'd look through a pane of window glass. Dan felt cold and afraid, and he couldn't continue to meet the marshal's stare. He looked down at his boots, shuffling them on the floor. "I got to go back and finish up my chores. I just thought I ought to tell you . . ."

He glanced up and found that the marshal's eyes were normal once again. Patch was tugging at his mustache and his smile was perfunctory. "Thanks, Dan. Thanks for coming down and telling me."

"What you goin' to do? You goin' to quit?"

Patch's eyes hardened suddenly. "Who told you to ask me that?" His voice was sharp, and the words snapped out.

"Nobody. Nobody told me to ask you nothin'." He edged toward the door. Patch was different this morning. It hadn't really been anything he said. It was just something that Dan felt.

Patch continued to tug at his mustache; his smile was gone. "All right, boy. All right. I'll see you after a while."

Dan escaped. Once outside the door, he ran toward the boardinghouse.

Frank Patch got up from his chair, walked to the door and watched Dan until he was out of sight. He glanced uneasily at the buildings across the street. A man with a rifle could hide on top of any one of them, he thought, and pick him off as he came out the front door of the jail. If the man's aim was good, he'd be dead before his hand could

54

touch his gun. Anyone who wanted to could pick him off at any time, from Sayre's warehouse or from any other vantage point. There was no sure defense against being ambushed.

He went back into his office in the front part of the jail. He sat down in his chair and lifted his booted feet to the top of the paper-littered desk.

It was not in the least unthinkable that someone might ambush him, particularly after the shooting of Luke Mills two weeks ago. Luke had tried to kill him. Now, with Luke's death supplying an additional reason, others might also try killing him.

He stared somberly around the office, at the things he had accumulated over the years, at the mementos of his twenty years in office here. He had a brief moment of doubt. Maybe he was out of date. Maybe he should resign.

Then he thought of Luke Mills, opening fire on him right on Elm Street in front of the Kansas Hotel two weeks ago. And he shook his head. Cottonwood Springs had not grown up. It was still the same as it had been twenty years ago. What did it matter whether shots were fired on its streets by drunken trail hands or by drunken residents of the town? Stray bullets killed innocent people no matter who fired them. Murder was murder no matter who committed it. The town still needed him, as much as it ever had.

Dan had said a delegation was coming to ask him to resign today. He'd have to try to convince them they were wrong. He'd have to convince them the town hadn't changed.

Chapter 5

They began to gather at a quarter of eight, the prominent men of the town, in the big back room at Sayre's Dry Goods Store. They came in the alley door because they didn't want to attract Patch's attention until they were ready for him.

Some of them acted scared. Others acted furtive. Still others seemed guilty, as though they were about to do something of which they were ashamed. But all were subdued. There was no hilarity and no boisterousness in their greetings to one another. In many cases a short nod sufficed for a greeting. In some, there was no greeting at all.

Chester Sayre was waiting for them, sitting at an old scarred desk. He nodded briefly as each came in. "Hello, Marv. Mornin', Andrew. How are you, Ivan?"

When eight o'clock came, there were fifteen men waiting there, fifteen of the town's leading citizens.

A buzz of talk now filled the room along with the smoke from their cigars and pipes. Sayre raised a hand. "All right. You know why we're here. It's been decided that we'll go down to the jail in a group and ask for Frank Patch's resignation as marshal of Cottonwood Springs." He let his glance roam over the group. "All the members of the town council are here, so in a sense it will be an official demand. To make it more so, I've put it in writing. I have signed it as mayor and I want each member of the town council to come up here and sign it too. Then we'll go on down to the jail with it."

"What if he won't quit?" This was the question that had been in all their minds. This was the question that had no answer – yet.

Sayre answered, "We don't know that he'll refuse to quit when the weight of the town is against him. We'll cross that bridge when we come to it."

Members of the town council edged to the front of the room to put their signatures beneath the mayor's on the demand.

Having done so, each council member shuffled aside to make room for someone else. When all the members of the town council had signed, Sayre picked up the paper, waved it in the air to dry the last signature, then carefully folded it and put it into the inside pocket of his coat.

All these men seemed reluctant, Sayre no less reluctant than the rest. His mouth firmed, and he walked to the front of the store, putting on his hat. The others followed, the town council coming along immediately behind, the others trailing raggedly.

In the street, Sayre marched toward the jail. The others shuffled after him, looking scared now that they were about to come face to face with Patch.

Sayre smiled grimly to himself. Such was the fear that Frank Patch inspired, such the respect. It explained why he was able to take lawbreakers into custody without even firing a shot. It explained how he was able to subdue a quarrelsome drunk without even striking a blow.

He began to feel ashamed of himself, as though he was one of a pack of wolves trying to bring down an old range bull. And, he admitted, that was exactly what he was, what all of them were. Wolves.

Patch was head and shoulders above the best of them. He'd faithfully performed his duties here in Cottonwood Springs for twenty years. He had made the town secure, had made its people unafraid. Outlaws gave Cottonwood Springs a wide berth simply because they knew that Patch was here. And how was the town repaying him? Then anger abruptly replaced the shame in Sayre. Why the hell did Patch have to be so stubborn about it?

Sayre's feeling of frustration increased. Now was the time for attracting new people to the town. The whole country was on the move, seemed like. Wichita was growing like a damned mushroom. Denver was a thriving metropolis. Along with new settlers, business and industry was moving west. If it weren't for Patch, Cottonwood Springs could be growing too.

Maybe they ought to pension him. Maybe if they did ... He stopped suddenly and whirled to face the others. He said, "Wait a minute. I've got an idea. What if we was to give him a little pension? Maybe then he'd quit."

Several of them looked at him as though he had lost his mind. Ivan Stanek said, "Pay him for nothing, for just sitting on his butt? Are you crazy, Ches? We got enough taxes as it is, and we'll have to pay the man who takes his place."

Sayre said sourly, "Men. No one man could take his place."

Stanek scowled. "You sound like you wanted to keep him on. What the hell's the matter with you anyway? Are you scared of him?"

"Maybe." Sayre smiled ruefully. "Maybe we all ought to be scared of him." He realized his suggestion had fallen on unreceptive ears. He turned and continued reluctantly toward the jail.

Reaching it, he crossed the small, untidy yard in front of it and pushed open the heavy door.

Patch, sitting at his desk with his feet on top of it, turned his head. Deliberately, he lowered his feet to the floor. He knew why they had come, but he gave no indication that he did. He raised his bushy eyebrows and stared at Sayre with cold, gray eyes. He said, "Well now, what's all this about?"

Sayre felt like a naughty little boy. He hadn't felt like this since he'd been called up in front of the class by the teacher nearly thirty years ago for putting a frog in Sarah Perkins' lard-pail lunch bucket. Instead of answering, Sayre reached into the inside pocket of his coat and withdrew the signed demand. He handed it to Patch, having to cross the room to the marshal to do so.

He felt his face grow red, felt sweat dampen his forehead and upper lip. Goddam Patch, anyway! Where the hell did he get off, making a man feel like this?

Patch read the demand in his deliberate, laborious way. When he had finished reading the last signature at the bottom of the page, he raised his eyes and looked steadily at the group. He looked at Sayre first, then at each of the others in their turn. His face was as nearly expressionless as it could get. If it showed anything at all, it showed contempt.

Patch didn't say anything. Deliberately, calmly, he ripped the paper in two, ripped it a second time and a third and fourth. He leaned over and dropped the torn fragments into the spittoon beside his desk. He glanced up at Sayre.

The marshal's eyes were coldly angry now; his face had gone white. His stare dared the mayor to protest. Sayre did not, but the others did. There was a sullen grumble of protest from several of them. Andrew Oxley said, "Damn it, you can't hold the job after you've been fired!"

Patch growled, "I thought I told you to keep out of this. I'm not going to warn you again."

Someone well hidden in the group mumbled audibly, "We hired you and we can fire you."

Patch searched the group, looking for the speaker, trying to single him out. Failing, he spoke directly to Sayre, who stood in front of them. "You were damned glad to get me twenty years ago. You were willing to promise me anything. Or have you forgotten that?"

Sayre did not reply so Patch went on. "I didn't ask for much. I didn't even ask the same wages they were getting in Wichita and Dodge. All I asked was what I'm getting now. And the job for as long as I wanted it. Well I still want it, gentlemen. I still want it and I'm going to hang onto it."

He waited a moment, staring at Sayre and at Oxley with both defiance and contempt. "Twenty years ago things weren't as tame as they are right now. Some of you remember even if the others don't. I laid my life on the line a dozen times the first month I worked for you. You ran up a debt to me every time I did." His eyes narrowed angrily. "Every time I pulled the trigger the debt got bigger. Do you think a man kills another man for a lousy seventy-five a month? Hell no, he don't."

Oxley spoke up with stubborn persistence. "If you didn't kill all those men for money, then why won't you quit? It sounds to me like the money's pretty all-fired important to you now."

Patch fixed his stare on Oxley. He said slowly and deliberately, "As long as we're talking about killing, I'll say this. All the men I killed had the bullet holes in front. And I never killed a man when I was drunk." He stopped, his expression a thinly veiled threat.

Oxley was silent now, his face

bloodless and almost gray. Sayre turned his head and glanced at him, startled by what he saw. Puzzled, he returned his gaze to Patch. "There's going to be trouble, Patch, if you won't quit. You know there'll be trouble over this."

Patch shrugged disinterestedly. "I can handle trouble. That's my job." His anger was no longer hot and furious. It had cooled to smoldering coals, but it had not completely gone away.

"We're not going to quit trying, Frank. There are other ways. There's the governor."

Patch's glance swept them all as he said harshly, angrily, "I know things about people in this town. I know things, lots of them, that they wouldn't want me to tell. And I can be pushed too far. I can be pushed into telling what I know." As though sensing danger, he straightened and shifted his position so that his hand was but inches from his holstered gun.

Sayre swung his head and glanced at Andrew Oxley. Oxley met his eyes and made a nervous, foolish smile. But Sayre had seen his expression before the smile had hidden it. Oxley was scared. Something Patch had said had scared the pants off him.

By the door someone muttered, "I think he's nuts. He ought to be put away."

Patch asked sharply, "Who said that?"

Nobody replied. Those at the rear of the group began to fade through the door. A general crowding began as those in front backed away from Patch.

Sayre said, "Think it over, will you, Frank? Give it some thought. I could probably get them to agree to some kind of pension for you if you'd quit."

Patch stared steadily at him. "How much?"

Sayre felt his face growing hot. He said, "Fifteen – maybe twenty dollars a month. With what you've got put away, you could make out pretty good."

Patch nodded. "I could get me a rockin' chair. I could sit and rock in the sun and maybe on good days I could get some kid to listen to me talk about how it was back in '68 when the trail herds were hitting town. Only there wouldn't be many days like that. I'd run out of new stories, and nobody would want to hear the old ones over and over again." He stopped, fished in his pocket for a cigar and carefully bit off the end. He said, "Nothing doing, Sayre. I got fifteen, maybe twenty years left in me. I ain't quittin' yet."

Sayre scowled and turned away. Oxley, ahead of him, pushed toward the door as though he couldn't get through it fast enough.

The delegation crowded out, silent until they had gone far enough so that Patch couldn't hear what was said. Then their voices broke into an outraged, angry babbling.

Sayre wondered why he couldn't take his eyes off Oxley's back. Oxley was headed up the street toward the office of the Star. He hadn't said a word since he'd pushed his way out of the jail.

Sayre watched him until he went into the newspaper office and slammed the door. Patch had something serious on Oxley. That was obvious. Something more serious than he had on most of the other men in town.

In his own case it was a woman – an affair that had been over for a long, long time but which would hurt him with Elizabeth just the same. In Oxley's case, it had to be something else.

Sayre headed for the dry goods store, aware that the others had turned downstreet toward the Alamo. He was frowning, wondering at the feeling of uneasiness that kept growing in his mind.

Chapter 6

Thirteen angry men filed into the Alamo Saloon. They crossed to the bar, and Ivan Stanek yelled at Lester Locke, who was behind the bar. "Give us a couple of bottles, Les," and slid a ten-dollar gold piece across the bar.

Locke put two bottles on the bar. He put a glass in front of each man. He stared at the men, knowing what they were mad about. Frank Patch had turned them down. He had refused to quit.

Locke was a middle-aged, bull-shouldered man. He was running to paunch these days, but he could still pick most men up bodily and throw them through the swinging doors into the street.

His head was almost completely bald except for a light fringe over his ears and on his neck. His skin was white because he stayed out of the sun. Unlike most of the other men strung out along the bar, Locke hated Patch.

It went back a long, long time. It went back to the time Patch nearly run Locke out of town for taking a cut from crooked gamblers and for trying to get a cut from the town's prostitutes. The hatred had persisted ever since, fed by real and imagined injustices. Like Patch's taking up with Claire Quintana, who owned the Goliad, thereby giving her an advantage over the other saloon-keepers in the town. Like Patch's permitting her to stay at the hotel on the other side of Texas Street while he made all the other saloonkeepers stay in quarters above their respective saloons.

Locke's hatred was a basic thing. If Patch was gone, Locke would be able to spread out. He could turn the Alamo into a gambling hall. He could import a dozen or more prostitutes. If Cotton-wood Springs grew as they said it would, he might end up with half a dozen brothels and two or three gambling halls. He could get mighty rich.

If **Patch** was gone. If. Locke listened to the angry talk, his eyes very cold and very hard. Locke wanted to see Patch lying dead in the street in a pool of his own coagulating blood. He wanted that more than anything else in the world.

Stanek, who had the town's biggest livery barn, said "Where the hell does he get off, anyway? We hired him and we've paid him all these years. We can fire him any time we want."

Locke made a tight, sarcastic grin. "Then why don't you fire him?"

Stanek's face flushed, and he glanced at Locke angrily. "Who told you to stick your goddam nose in this?"

Locke's blue eyes narrowed. He said in clipped, angry tones, "Don't get uppity with me. I run a business in this town and I pay taxes just like any of the rest of you."

Stanek's expression moderated. He said, "Oh hell, I'm sorry, Les. I didn't mean to snap at you. It's just that Patch has us so damned stirred up. We just tried to fire him and we didn't get anywhere."

"What'd he say?"

"He said no. That's all he had to say. And what the hell can the town do about it?"

Locke thought of Lou Trinidad, the county sheriff. He said, "Maybe Lou Trinidad could get up a posse and take care of him. Maybe Lou could throw him in jail and charge him with obstructing justice or something."

Stanek seemed to consider the proposal briefly. Then he shook his head. "Lou hasn't got what it takes to go up against Patch and that's what he'd be doing, no matter how big a posse he had to back him up."

Locke realized that what Stanek said was true. Rosenbloom said, "Maybe we ought to just forget about it. Maybe we ought to let him stay on the job. If we keep pushing, somebody's liable to get hurt."

Both Stanek and Locke glanced at

Rosenbloom. Stanek asked, "Why should anybody get hurt?"

There was silence along the bar for several moments while one after another of the men gulped their drinks. Locke glanced along the bar, looking at their faces one by one. They were scared. They were beginning to realize how impossible this situation was. For the first time, they were considering the alternative, shooting Patch.

Not that they would actually try killing him themselves. One or two of them were capable of it, of course, if circumstances were right and if the provocation was great enough. But most of them would only think about it.

His face twisted almost imperceptibly. They'd think about it, these solid, respectable citizens. They'd think about it, and if it happened they would already have accepted it. They'd condone it because there wasn't any other way to stop Patch from holding back the progress of the town, thereby hurting them in their wretched pocketbooks.

The talk went on, and Locke listened, but with only a part of his mind. His eyes were brighter than usual, and there was a light film of perspiration on the top of his bald head.

He had no plan as yet but he was groping for one that would work. The town was almost ready to condone the killing of Frank Patch. He'd better be ready with his plan when the right time came. He suddenly felt as excited as a boy at the prospect of being rid of Patch at last.

Andrew Oxley slammed into the front office of the Cottonwood Star and banged the door shut after him. He could hear the hand press going on in back, where Will was printing up the weekly edition of the newspaper.

Forcing himself to be calm and deliberate, Oxley hung up his hat on the coat tree just beside the door. He wiped his forehead with his hand, then crossed the room to the open door leading to the pressroom in the back.

Will did not look up. There was a light frown of concentration on his face as he worked.

Andrew Oxley stared at him almost hungrily. He forced himself to turn away, forced himself to cross the room and sit down at his desk.

Damn Patch anyway! Damn Frank Patch to hell! His oblique reference back there in the marshal's office to shooting men only from the front, and only when he was sober.... Oxley knew what he'd meant even if no one else had known. And the warning Patch had issued earlier down by the hanging tree. Oxley had understood that, too.

Patch had been threatening him, blackmailing him openly and flagrantly. Patch had been saying, as clearly as if he had said it in so many words, that Oxley had better disassociate himself from those trying to fire him or he'd spill everything he knew.

The consequences would be terrible if he did. Oxley frowned with quiet desperation. He couldn't bear to think of the consequences. He couldn't bear to think of the way Will would look at him once the truth was known.

He went back to the pressroom and glanced in again at Will. He felt as if a cold hand was squeezing on his heart. If Patch felt cornered enough to threaten him today, he might feel cornered enough to expose him to the town tomorrow. Besides, even if he did withdraw from the movement to oust Patch from his job, how would Patch know he had withdrawn? Would Patch tell?

A sudden, shocking thought occurred to him. There was one way to end the doubt. Maybe he ought to finish what Luke Mills had started two weeks ago. Maybe there was only one way to be absolutely sure Frank Patch didn't give him away. Maybe he ought to kill Patch himself and bury with him forever the things that only Frank Patch knew. His mind conjured up an image of Patch, solid, strong, so everlastingly confident and sure of himself. How could he kill a man like that?

He groaned with the horror of his thoughts. He was actually thinking of committing murder. Was that the way it had been the other time?

He tried to stop thinking, but he could no longer control his thoughts. He could kill Patch in only one way. From ambush or from behind. Otherwise he'd be killed himself.

His hands were trembling, and his whole body was clammy and cold. His teeth were chattering as though he had a chill. He returned to his desk, praying that Will wouldn't come in and find him like this. Will would think he was sick, and he'd have a hell of a time convincing the boy he was not.

He couldn't afford to be sick. He couldn't afford weakness, or chills, or fear. If he was going to go through with killing Patch today, it would take every bit of strength and courage he possessed. But once it was done ... once it was done, he could stop worrying forever. No one but Patch knew the truth. No one but Patch could expose him, could expose what he had done so long ago.

His eyes narrowed with what almost seemed to be physical pain. But the pain was not physical. It was the anguish of remembering.

It happened in '72. It had happened less than half a dozen miles from Cottonwood Springs, out on the vast, Kansas prairie that could have hidden a hundred worse crimes and probably had.

Oxley had been traveling West. He had been a young man then, with a lot of big ideas. He had wanted to start a newspaper somewhere in the West. But one day, miles from anywhere, his horse had just lain down and died.

Not knowing whether he was near any settlement, Oxley continued on foot, hungry, near exhaustion and thoroughly scared. He came unexpectedly on a wagon with a man driving, a two-year-old boy riding solemnly beside him on the seat. The man had buried his wife fifty miles back and said he was now trying to find a town and someone to take care of the child.

He was a thoroughly unpleasant man, dirty and smelly and foul-mouthed. Oxley had the feeling the man would leave the boy on the prairie to die if he did not find someone to take him soon.

That night, while the boy slept in the wagon, the man brought out a stoneware jug of whiskey. He and Oxley began to drink, with Oxley reluctant to refuse not only because he was grateful to the man for the ride but also because he was afraid of him.

He wasn't too clear on what happened afterward. He vaguely remembered a quarrel when he regained consciousness next day. He found a gun with two cylinders fired beside him and not far away the body of the man with two bullets in his back. The boy was still asleep in the wagon bed.

Oxley didn't know what to do. He'd begun to dig a grave, when Patch arrived, riding his big black horse, his eyes holding only contempt for what appeared to be a back-shooting murder.

Oxley didn't remember all that had been said. He did remember trying to convince Patch that he had not intended to kill anyone, that he had not coveted the man's wagon and killed him for it. He did convince Patch that nothing was to be gained by hanging him, that the child, a boy, would be the marshal's sole responsibility if he did. Oxley promised to keep the boy and raise him under the marshal's eye if Patch would only forget what had happened here.

He still didn't quite know why Patch had agreed. Perhaps it was because the marshal knew of no one who would take the child. Cottonwood Springs, at that time, contained few good women, and apparently none of them were willing to take on the responsibility of an orphan child.

Perhaps Oxley had convinced Patch that he could raise the child successfully himself. Perhaps he had only offered Patch a way out of a dilemma. Patch might even have believed the story that he told. Anyway Patch knew he could

81

ruin him at any time if he did not do right by the boy.

Fortunately, the child was healthy, with a constitution that could weather almost anything. He grew like a weed and he filled Andrew Oxley's empty life until he became the most important part of it.

Patch had watched approvingly. He had never threatened to expose Oxley until today. And, Oxley realized, the marshal would not have threatened today had not his back been against a wall.

But it didn't matter what made Patch threaten to tell the truth. What mattered was that he had it in his power not only to ruin Oxley but also to drive young Will away. What young man could continue to respect someone he discovered had shot his father in the back? It would be shock enough for Will to discover that Oxley was not his father at all. But to discover also that Oxley had killed his real father in a drunken fight and by shooting him in the back . . .

Cold and sweating, Oxley got up suddenly from his desk. Once more he walked silently to the door leading to the pressroom and looked at Will. Will glanced up and smiled and went back to his work.

He was a tall, slenderly built young man. Andrew Oxley felt his throat tighten up as he watched. He turned away suddenly. With a firm step, he walked to the door, opened it and went into the street. He had a gun at home. He had a rifle he had hunted deer with years ago.

He walked as far as the intersection of Texas and Elm streets. Here he stopped. He was insane to think of killing Patch. Then he shook his head. The town wasn't going to stop trying to get Patch to quit. And when the pressure became great enough, Patch would strike back in any way he could. He'd blame Oxley for being a part of it, and he'd tell everything he knew . . .

He stared at the marshal's office, then let his gaze cross the street to the buildings facing it. There was one, a two-story, red-brick building directly across from the jail. In the lower story it housed a saddle shop run by a man named Olaf Pedersen and, next to that, a warehouse used by Chester Sayre. The upper story was vacant now, though it still bore the painted legend on its windows. "Lucas Carr, Attorney at Law." Carr had died nearly a decade before, and the office hadn't been rented since, probably because it was below Texas Street.

There was an outside stairway leading up from the street in front, but most of the steps were missing and it was unusable. But Oxley thought he recalled a rear stairway, too . . .

He crossed Elm and walked along Texas Street to the alley. He glanced behind him, and all around guiltily. He went quickly into the alley mouth, hurrying.

Behind the red-brick building, he stopped. There was, indeed, a rear stairway leading up. It looked dilapidated and rickety but it was better than the one in front. Oxley pushed open a sagging gate and went into the weed-infested yard behind the building. He threaded his way carefully, occasionally glancing furtively around to see if he was being watched.

He reached the foot of the stairs. He climbed them carefully. At the top there was a door in which the glass was broken. Oxley reached through the broken pane and unbolted it. He went inside.

He could hear mice scurrying, and there was a musty smell about the place. Dust and dry leaves lay on the floor along with scraps of torn paper and even some feathers from long dead birds. Oxley walked along the short hallway and opened a door on which Lucas Carr's name was still visible. He crossed the dusty, vacant room to the window, which faced the street.

From here, he could clearly see the marshal's office and the jail. The window glass was very dirty but he did not try to clean a space. He'd either have to open the window a little bit or break it when the time came. But he could kill Patch from here if his aim was good. And his aim ought to be good at a range of no more than fifty or sixty feet.

He retraced his steps, carefully closing the office door, carefully closing the outer door and bolting it, even though the glass was out. He went cautiously down the stairs.

There was only one thing wrong with using Carr's old office for ambushing Patch. He'd be caught up there like a rat in a trap. If he didn't succeed in killing Patch, he wouldn't have a chance of escaping the marshal's wrath. He'd be trapped, unable to go down the front stairway into the street, surely blocked from going down the rear stairway by Patch himself.

He hesitated in the deserted rear yard of the building, glancing around confusedly. Finally, seeing a passageway between the red-brick building and the next building, he picked his way to it and entered it.

It was a narrow passageway, no more than a foot wide. He had to sidle along it, rather than walking squarely because his shoulders scraped both sides. That was good, he thought. Patch was almost twice as broad as he. Patch would be slower negotiating it than he.

The passageway was littered with tin cans and trash. He picked his way slowly and silently along it almost to the street.

Here he stopped, motionless. He could see the door of Patch's office from here. He could also shoot from here.

And the passageway had an added advantage. It would not be spotted immediately as his hiding place because the smoke from his gun would not be immediately visible the way it would be if he fired on Patch from the office overhead. He could stay far enough back in the passageway so that the powder-smoke would not show in the street until he'd had time to go back along the passageway and disappear.

Satisfied, he retraced his steps, returned to the alley and walked along it to Texas Street. He kept looking around furtively, but he saw no one.

Once he had reached Texas Street, he walked swiftly and openly toward home. He began to feel cold again and he began to sweat, but he kept walking steadily. He knew what he had to do. Patch might have his back against the wall, but so did he.

Yet in spite of his decision to do what he thought had to be done, a pervading horror remained in his thoughts. He had killed before, but he had always been able to tell himself it had been an accident. This time it would be murder, cold-blooded and terrible. He nearly stopped himself. Then he thought of the look that would come into young Will's eyes when he knew what the man he thought was his father had done. And resolutely Oxley continued on toward home.

Chapter 7

Frank Patch watched the angry townsmen leave, not missing the way they waited until they were out of earshot before they began talking excitedly among themselves. He knew what they were saying, knew at least the gist of it. He watched until they disappeared, most of them going downstreet toward the saloons, only Oxley and Sayre heading uptown in the same direction from which they had come earlier.

He was sorry about some of the things he had said. But what the hell was a man supposed to do, he asked himself angrily. Was he supposed to stand meekly aside while they replaced him with someone who didn't know the first thing about doing his job, about doing the job he'd always done so well?

He began pacing nervously. He began

to think of Oxley, and his face felt hot as he remembered what he had said to the man. He hadn't intended to taunt Oxley with something that had happened more than sixteen years ago, and he would never, no matter what happened, tell Will Oxley that the man he thought was his father had, in reality, shot his father in the back when Will was only two years old.

Patch admired Oxley. He'd never regretted helping Oxley bury the man out on the prairie in an unmarked grave. He'd never regretted keeping his mouth shut about the crime.

It had turned out exactly the way he'd hoped it would that day, and it had probably turned out a lot better for the boy than if it had not happened. The boy's father certainly hadn't looked like much, even when he was dead.

Frowning, Patch wondered why he had done what he had that day. He had only been marshal of Cottonwood Springs, true, without authority outside the limits of the town. But he'd never hewed to that line and never would. No, it had been something else. Something about Oxley, himself, perhaps. Something about the way the little boy had run to him when he awoke.

Returning to the window, Patch stared in the direction in which Oxley had disappeared. He ought to go up there and apologize to Oxley for the remark he'd made. Shrugging, he put the thought away from him temporarily. Plenty of time to apologize. Right now he had more important things to think about.

What would they do next? Sayre had mentioned the governor, but Patch didn't know what the hell the governor could do short of declaring an insurrection and sending in the state militia to put him out of his job.

He smiled grimly to himself at the thought of a company of militia marching down Elm Street and drawing up in formation outside his office. His grin widened as he imagined what their commander might say to him. Then the grin faded. It would never come to that. They'd find some other way before it went that far.

But what other way? Would they get Lou Trinidad to get up a posse and try to oust him by arresting him? He doubted it. Lou Trinidad didn't have the courage to face up to him. He'd been out on posses with the sheriff a time or two and hadn't found Trinidad exactly reckless about exposing himself to gunfire from a fugitive.

Should he quit? Every time he thought of it, his whole spine turned cold. It would kill him to be idle. It would kill him to sit in a rocking chair and watch while the world passed by. He was too young for that anyway. There were fifteen or twenty good years left in him.

Back and forth he paced. Back and forth, like a lion in a cage. Dan Joslyn came hurrying down the street, turned in at the gate and opened the office door. Dan's eyes were excited and there was a film of sweat on his face. He closed the door behind him and faced the marshal, who had stopped pacing when he came in. "What happened, Mr. Patch?"

"Happened?" Patch grinned wryly at the boy. "The mayor and a delegation of citizens came down here to demand that I resign."

"What'd you tell 'em, Mr. Patch?"

"I told them no."

Dan's eyes shone, giving Patch an abundance of approval. But the boy didn't speak. He just stood there awkwardly, shifting from one foot to the other. At last he asked, "What's going to happen now?"

Patch shrugged ponderously. "I don't know, Dan. I don't know. I guess they'll try to think of something else."

Dan fidgeted a moment more. Then he said, "Well, I got to go. I just wondered how things came out."

"Thanks for coming, Dan."

"Sure, Mr. Patch." Dan went out, ran uptown toward Jorgensen's boarding-house and disappeared; Patch began to pace again.

Dan was gone less than ten minutes.

When he came back, he looked both uncertain and a little scared. Patch asked, "Forget something, Dan?"

Dan shook his head. "I just wondered . . . you reckon Mr. Oxley would be going hunting today?"

"Hunting? Why?"

"I just saw him leavin' his house with a rifle in his hands."

Patch said, "No. He wouldn't be going hunting, Dan. Maybe he's just taking his gun down to have it fixed."

Dan nodded and turned back toward the door. "I just thought you ought to know. Just in case . . ." He left the sentence dangling.

Patch nodded. He didn't speak, but he could tell Dan had guessed what was in Andrew Oxley's mind even though Dan didn't know what Oxley's provocation was.

Patch watched the boy go reluctantly out the door and cursed softly beneath his breath. He'd been a fool. He'd let his anger get the best of him, and he'd said things he hadn't meant and had never intended to say. This was the result.

He glanced across the street, at the dirty office windows over Sayre's warehouse and the saddle shop next door. He glanced at the roof and he wondered where Oxley would stand when he used the rifle Dan had seen him carrying.

A feeling of fatalism, of events marching to a deadly climax long ago ordained, came over him, settling like a heavy weight in his thoughts. It began two weeks ago, he thought, when he shot Luke Mills. That was when the agitation to remove him had started in earnest. That was when it had really become serious. It had grown with each passing day until today. And it was growing ever more rapidly now. He'd been threatened, however obliquely, by the boarders at Jorgensen's. Now Oxley had a rifle and was really hunting him.

Patch paced back and forth for five minutes more, scowling, trying to decide the best thing for him to do. At last he slammed out the door. He untied his horse, mounted and rode down the street. Nothing would be gained by hiding in the marshal's office. If Oxley were going to shoot him, he'd shoot him no matter where the marshal was. And maybe by thus exposing himself, maybe by letting Oxley know he wasn't in the least afraid, Patch could discourage the man. Oxley wasn't a killer. He wasn't a man of violence. If Oxley had pulled the trigger sixteen years ago and had killed Will's father by shooting him in the back, the shooting must have been some kind of bizarre accident. Patch knew that now, even if he hadn't been wholly sure of it then.

He forced himself to keep his eyes straight ahead, ignoring the red-brick building across the street. He rode toward the railroad tracks, and as he rode, a little spot in the middle of his back began to ache.

It took all the willpower he had to look casual and unconcerned. But he managed to do so. He looked exactly as he had a hundred, a thousand times before, setting out to make his rounds.

He looked as though he wasn't afraid of anything.

Dan Joslyn did not go home to Jorgensen's boardinghouse when he left Patch the second time, because Dan thought he knew what Oxley was carrying his rifle for. Oxley meant to try to shoot Patch.

Why Andrew Oxley should want to shoot Patch, Dan couldn't imagine, but then Dan didn't begin to understand the strange and sometimes devious ways of adults. He did know Oxley wasn't going hunting. Not today. And he knew Oxley wouldn't make a special trip home for his rifle just to have it fixed.

He saw Patch come from the office door and mount his horse. He was heading out to make his rounds of the town again, just as he had a thousand times before, but Dan understood, as Patch did, that this was more than just making his rounds. He was daring Oxley to shoot him.

Dan felt his throat choke up as he

stared at Patch's broad, heavily muscled back. In this moment, Patch seemed like a god to him, riding so slowly down the street, not even bothering to look at the warehouse building across the street from which he surely knew the shot would come.

But Dan looked at the building across the street. He searched its roof, searched each dirty, second-floor window before he let his glance come down to search the warehouse windows and the windows of the saddle shop. He saw the narrow passageway between the red-brick building and the building next to it and sidled along the street until he could see the length of the passageway. It was empty now. But it would make a good hiding place for anyone who wanted to shoot Patch.

By now, Patch was halfway to the depot. The trouble was, Dan thought as he followed him, there were a hundred places where an ambusher could hide. And Patch made a mighty good target, sitting up there on his big black horse, a target it would be hard to miss.

Patch rode all the way down Elm to the depot. He crossed the tracks, his horse picking his way daintily over the ties and tracks and cinder beds, rode past the loading pens, now gray and weathered and sagging in disrepair. Dan continued to follow, staying out of sight when possible, hurrying when he had nothing behind which to hide. But Patch did not look around.

It wasn't only Oxley the marshal was showing himself for, Dan thought. He was showing himself for the entire town. He was showing his contempt. Down in the middle of the maze of cattle pens, Frank Patch stopped. He sat his horse, glancing around him at the graying wreckage of the past.

Dan stared at his face from a distance of fifty feet. And suddenly it was as though this were twenty years ago, as though these pens were filled with bawling long-horned Texas cattle, as though the alleyways between the pens were crowded with shaggy, yelling Texas men on shaggy, short-legged cow ponies. It was as though a brass-stacked engine were noisily tugging cattle cars into position at the loading chutes.

There was dust, and bustle, and all kinds of noise. There was excitement; there were the smells of sagebrush and manure, of horse sweat and man sweat; and there was the heady feeling of being a part of history. Dan had sat and had listened to Frank Patch talk many winter nights, and these things were made almost as real by Patch's stories of them as they were real in Patch's mind.

But the visions faded, and there remained only Patch, sitting alone on his big black horse. There were only the graying, decaying cattle pens, and the deserted railroad station that would remain deserted until the noon train came in. There was the town beyond, the town that wanted to forget its lusty past and put on the white collar of progress and grow civilized. There was the town that might have to kill the past before it could become civilized.

Patch rode on, threading his way through the cattle pens and dropping into the bed of Cottonwood Creek beyond. Dan ran to keep up now, but he stayed on the lip of the ravine so that Patch wouldn't know he was following him.

From a distance, he saw Patch stop beneath the towering, golden-leafed cottonwood. He saw Patch stare up somberly at the stout, horizontal limb from which so many men had been hanged.

And he had a strange feeling, suddenly, that Patch was preparing himself for death. He was revisiting, perhaps for the last time, all the places that loomed so large in his memory, the places that meant so much to him.

Once again Dan's throat felt tight. His thoughts cried out, "Don't let them do it, Mr. Patch! You can stop 'em if you try, but you've got to try!"

Patch stayed beneath the cotton-wood for a long, long time. Then, almost reluctantly, he put his horse up the steep

101

bank of the ravine. He rode along Goodnight Street toward Elm, with Dan
trotting along behind, keeping pace but
staying out of sight.

Chapter 8

Andrew Oxley did not realize that he had been observed leaving home with the rifle in his hands. He would not have cared if he had. He had reached the point where consequences had been weighed against what must be done and put aside as of no importance any more. Frank Patch had threatened him. Patch had threatened his relationship with young Will, a thing more important to Andrew Oxley than his life. Now he would do what had to be done. He would kill Patch, if he could.

He carried the rifle with the muzzle pointing down, and held it tight against his leg as he walked so that it would not be noticed unless the observer was pretty close to him. There was no use advertising the fact that he was carrying it.

He had prepared himself for the consequences of what he meant to do. He would be arrested, of course, and brought to trial. He might even be convicted and sentenced to prison. But it was doubtful if he would hang. It was doubtful if any jury selected from men of Cottonwood Springs would decree that he should hang.

He had to cross Elm carrying the rifle and he realized how dangerous doing so could be. So he worked his way all the way downtown to the railroad tracks and crossed down there, still holding the rifle against his leg, moving it with his leg so that it would not be noticeable. He reached the far side of the street unobserved and began to work his way back uptown along the alley between A Street and Elm. He saw Patch ride past along Elm heading for the railroad tracks and a few moments afterward saw young Dan Joslyn following him.

Oxley crouched in the weeds until the two had disappeared from sight, then he went on, moving slowly and cautiously, until he reached the rear of the red-brick building facing the jail and directly across the street from it.

He made his way through the weeds and trash hurriedly, hoping no one would see him now. He entered the passageway and picked his way along it until he could see the jail and the door to Patch's office in front of it.

Now he kicked a place clear where he was standing and crouched on his heels, bracing himself against the walls on both sides of him. He raised the rifle and laid his cheek against the stock.

The sights lined up on Patch's office door, lined up and steadied there. Oxley held his breath, pleased that bracing himself this way had stilled his shaking hands. He would kill Patch from here; it would be hard to miss.

All he could do now was wait until Patch returned; until he tied his horse out front and walked through that sagging gate to his office door. All Oxley could do now was wait.

Patch knew Dan was following him. He also knew why. So he pretended not to see the boy, pretended not to notice him. His lips broke into a slight, steady smile. It is good to have someone worry about you, no matter how strong, no matter how competent you think you are.

Thinking about Dan, Patch realized suddenly what Sayre had realized earlier. He had no friends, no friends among adults. He had only Dan, and perhaps Clair, if it would be proper to think of Claire as a friend.

This realization depressed him suddenly. By the time he was middle-aged, a man ought to have friends. He ought to know other men who understood the way he felt about things, who knew the way he thought.

It was his own fault. He had built a wall around himself; he had drawn a line as plain as the one he had drawn twenty years ago down the middle of Texas Street. He had served notice on the rest of humanity that this line was not to be crossed.

Even those close to him had not been allowed to cross the line, not Claire, not even Dan. He had never really let them know what made Frank Patch tick. He sudenly did not like himself very much. Yet he knew he could not change. A man is the product of his environment. The things he experiences and feels and lives are the things that mold his character. If he sees evil as a child, he believes in evil as a man. If he knows harshness as a child, he will be a man who is both harsh and forever alone. If a man is to love, he must first learn love as a child. And Patch had never learned.

Patch reached the intersection of Goodnight and Elm streets and stopped, staring up and down Elm, feeling once more that strange sore spot in the middle of his back. He had given Oxley time to position himself and get set. Oxley would shoot before he reached his office door.

Patch's state of mind seemed to communicate itself to the horse, through the tenseness in his legs, through the way he balanced himself so lightly against the stirrups, perhaps through a strange understanding that had grown up over the years between the two. The horse pranced briefly, then seemed to steady down. Yet Patch could feel the tenseness in the horse as plainly as the horse had felt the tenseness in him. He reined the horse aside and started down the street toward his office in the jail.

Where would the shots come from, Patch asked himself. From nearby, or from long range, from beyond the range of the revolver at his side?

From nearby, he told himself. From nearby, because Oxley wasn't much of a shot with any kind of gun. Oxley wouldn't risk missing with his first shot. He'd find a place that was very close.

Patch's eyes lifted unobtrusively to the roof of the building across the street from the jail. He watched several moments but caught no movement there. His eyes ranged lower, searching the dirty windows of the offices that had formerly been occupied by Lucas Carr.

He couldn't see through the windows, but they were unbroken and intact. If Oxley was waiting there, he'd have to smash a window before he could shoot. And that would give Patch the split second he needed to survive.

The roof or the windows. It had to be one of the two places because no other vantage point was quite close enough. Without seeming to, Patch glanced behind, turning his head only enough to catch the quick movement of Dan Joslyn following. Dan was almost half a block behind. Dan would be safe enough, no matter what happened in the next minute or two.

The horse felt like a coiled steel spring against the marshal's legs. The animal's neck was arched, his ears pricked, his nostrils flared. Patch watched the horse's ears, knowing they would point out Oxley's hiding place if the man moved or made the slightest noise. Patch's hand, though seeming to rest indolently against his thigh, was as tense as the horse, as tense as the rest of him. A step at a time the horse paced down the street.

Past the passageway. Past the place where Oxley was hiding. And as the marshal passed, Oxley moved the rifle slightly to follow Patch with its sights.

The horse's eyes rolled, though he did not turn his head. The horse's ears pricked toward the sound.

Patch knew instantly where Oxley was. He also knew Oxley probably wouldn't shoot, now, until Patch had drawn the horse to a halt, until he sat momentarily motionless in front of his office across the street.

He reined the horse aside, pointing him toward the tie-rail, and came to a sudden halt just short of it.

He left the saddle in a shallow dive, swinging his right foot over the horse's neck and pushing against the stirrup with his left. He heard the crack of the rifle reverberating from the narrow passageway just as he hit the dusty street, rolling, his gun already in his hand.

The horse danced nervously away,

head turned so that he would not step on the trailing reins, eyes rolling wildly toward the sound of the sudden shot, toward the cloud of powdersmoke billowing into the street from the mouth of the passageway.

Patch stopped rolling and gathered his feet under him, leaping up, plunging across the street toward the shelter of the building wall. Again the rifle roared, and this bullet tore a furrow in the dust at his feet, a little in front of him. It showered him with fine dust, momentarily filling his eyes with it, momentarily blinding him.

Almost wholly blind, he plunged across the street and slammed into the building wall with an impact that shook him and almost made him drop his gun. He knuckled his streaming eyes with his left hand, blinking them, desperately trying to clear them so that he could see. Oxley would probably not shoot again, Patch thought. Oxley would be unnerved by the failure of his first two shots. But Patch couldn't be sure. He couldn't be sure how desperate Oxley was.

Through his swimming, dirt-filled eyes, Patch saw Oxley come into sight at the mouth of the passageway. He saw the man swing the rifle and bring it up. . . .

Patch's actions were automatic now, instinctive, because it was defend himself or die. His revolver came into line. He didn't have to see its sights. He didn't have to aim. All he had to do was see what he intended to shoot.

Oxley's shot and Patch's sounded almost simultaneously. A little plume of smoke curled up ·from the muzzle of Patch's gun.

Smoke billowed out from Oxley's gun, momentarily hiding the man from Patch's view. It drifted slowly away on the wind.

There was a look of surprise and unbelief on Oxley's face. He stared at Patch while the gun slipped from his hands into the dust at his feet. He stood this way for an instant, bent forward a little as though he had a stomach ache.

Patch started toward him, shoving the gun into the holster at his side. He said, "Mr. Oxley, you didn't have to do this."

He didn't know whether Oxley understood or not. The man folded quietly, knees first, so that he fell in a little heap where he had been standing only an instant before. His face went down in the dust before Patch could reach him.

Patch dimly heard a shout uptown. He dimly heard the sound of running feet. It was just as it had been two weeks ago when Luke Mills had tried to kill him out in front of the Kansas Hotel at night. He had killed another townsman.

He reached Oxley and knelt. He gently turned the man over and almost automatically picked up his wrist. There was a pulse, but it was weak. From Oxley's chest, rising and falling almost imperceptibly, he glanced up at Oxley's face. He didn't have to look for the wound; he knew where that was, even before blood began to soak the front of Oxleys' shirt.

Oxley opened his eyes. There was a

smudge of dust on his chin, dust that had turned to mud on his lips. He stared up at Patch. He said, "It's numb, Frank. It doesn't hurt."

Patch nodded.

Oxley asked, "What's going to happen to Will? You won't tell . . .?"

Patch shook his head. "I won't tell. You have my word."

Oxley made a faint, small smile. "I've been a fool. I thought you would tell. I got scared, Frank."

Patch said, "We all get scared sometimes." He felt Oxley's hand groping. He took it in his own and knew by the way it gripped that Oxley was feeling pain now from the wound. Oxley gasped, and his breathing became shallower. He looked straight at Patch and asked, "How long, Frank? How long?"

Patch said, "A few minutes, Mr. Oxley."

"How're you going to explain me taking a shot at you?"

Patch frowned. He didn't know.

Oxley's hand gripped tighter than

before. "You won't tell the truth?"

Patch shook his head. "I'll think of something, Mr. Oxley, but it won't be the truth."

He became aware of someone standing a dozen feet away, staring silently. He glanced up and saw that it was Dan. Behind Dan, others were coming, running at first, their pace slowing to a walk as they came close. Dan said in a voice that was barely audible, "Mr. Patch, is he hurt bad? You want me to get some help?"

Patch shook his head. He said, "Go home, Dan. There's nothing you can do."

"What'd he mean when he asked if you were going to tell the truth?"

Patch's eyes grew hard. His voice was suddenly stern and cold. "You forget about that, boy. Don't you repeat it, you understand?"

"Yes sir." Dan's face looked white and scared. He lingered for just a moment more, then turned and ran toward home.

Oxley was still alive, but now his eyes

were closed. His breathing was very shallow and very weak.

Patch began to curse, softly, bitterly, beneath his breath. Oxley opened his eyes and stared up at him. Patch said, "Mr. Oxley, I didn't want to do this."

Oxley nodded but he didn't speak. Then his breathing stopped, and his eyes lost their look of life.

Patch closed them, one by one. He released Oxley's hand and got stiffly to his feet. He was cursing again, softly but with increasing bitterness.

He stared at the townsmen standing in a group watching him. There was rage in his eyes, anger that silenced instantly whatever any of them might have wanted to say. He stalked across to his horse. He mounted the animal and suddenly spurred away down the street. He thundered across the railroad tracks and in minutes disappeared into the rolling prairie beyond the town.

Chapter 9

Dan Joslyn ran for a block and a half before he stopped. He felt almost sick, as though someone had hit him in the stomach or he'd eaten too many green apples all at once. Everything seemed to be going wrong. Everything seemed to be going wrong at once.

It seemed unbelievable to Dan that Mr. Oxley would try to kill Frank Patch, but he couldn't doubt his eyes. It had happened and it had been no accident. Mr. Oxley had ambushed Patch, fully intending to murder him. But why?

No one could blame Frank Patch for killing him. No one could blame the marshal for defending himself. It had been the same as two weeks ago when Patch had killed Luke Mills. He'd just been defending himself. Hadn't he?

A doubt had entered Dan Joslyn's

mind. Something was wrong; something was terribly wrong. Both Luke Mills and Mr. Oxley had been decent, responsible citizens. It didn't seem possible that both had actually tried to kill the marshal right on Elm Street in front of everyone.

Dan stared back in the direction from which he had just come. Patch was gone. His horse had disappeared beyond a rise of ground just outside the town. There was a growing crowd down in front of the jail. Someone came running into the newspaper office, and a moment later Will Oxley came out. Walking almost dazedly, he went down the dusty street to the place where his father lay.

Some men carried Oxley's limp body toward his home over on Oak Street near the upper end of town. Will Oxley walked dazedly behind, still wearing the apron he wore when he was working the press and printing the weekly newspaper. They passed Dan less than twenty feet away, and he suddenly felt as if his chest and stomach were just one big empty hollow place. He wanted to throw

118

up. He wanted to cry but his eyes stayed dry.

For a little while the men of the town stayed there in front of the jail. They made a group, talking among themselves, sometimes gesticulating with their hands. Dan didn't have to hear their talk to know what it was about.

He stared over their heads at the horizon beyond the town where Patch had disappeared. More than anything in the world, right now, he wanted to talk to Patch. He wanted to be reassured by the marshal's calm, steady voice, by his wise, sure eyes. He wanted to hear Patch speak of what had happened in his matter-of-fact tones so that the event would become commonplace and less horrible in Dan's mind. But Patch was gone. He had ridden out onto the prairie beyond the town.

Dan turned and shuffled toward the boardinghouse. Reaching the steps, he sat down. And suddenly he began to cry, in great, long shuddering sobs that shook him from head to foot.

Patch rode recklessly for half a mile until concern for the horse made him draw the animal to a walk. The horse's neck gleamed with sweat and he was breathing hard. The black wasn't in condition for a run, he thought. He was too old and fat these days for this sort of thing.

Patch was scowling angrily and felt an unaccustomed sense of loss. He'd liked Andrew Oxley and had respected him. He hadn't meant for it to turn out this way. He'd only been trying to defend himself and his right to the marshal's job. There was no reason why he should have to take all the blame. After all, Andrew Oxley had deliberately ambushed him. Oxley had fired two shots at him before he fired back.

He halted the black and absently stroked the animal's sweating neck. He stared back toward the town, a grim expression of self-derision on his face. He'd never let killing a lawbreaker shake him up this way before. He supposed the reason he was so shaken now was that he'd known Andrew Oxley so well. Or he'd thought he had. He hadn't thought Oxley capable of any kind of violence.

He turned the horse's head toward town and rode back at a slow walk. He was needed in Cottonwood Springs right now. He was needed to keep the hotheads in line. There would be a lot of reckless talk going around back there, talk about getting rid of him, maybe talk about setting up an ambush that wouldn't fail as Oxley's ambush had.

The crowd was still in front of the jail when he rode in. They raised their faces and stared at him sullenly, then shuffled away toward the Alamo Saloon. It was notable the way they avoided the Goliad. Patch wondered suddenly where Claire was and what she thought of him. He wondered if she was also condemning him and supposed she was. She'd never tell him if she was. She'd keep her disapproval to herself. But he'd feel it. He'd feel it because she wouldn't be able to hide it successfully.

On impulse he returned to the Goliad, dismounted and looped the reins around the rail. He went in through the double swinging doors, pushing his hat back on his head as he did. Claire turned from the window where she had been standing, looking into the street. She didn't speak, but her eyes were soft and there was a suspicious brightness in them.

Patch said, "Good morning, Claire," and walked across to the bar. Jake, the bartender, looked at him expectantly. Patch was about to order a bottle of whiskey and a glass but stopped himself. Instead he ordered beer. He needed a clear head today. He needed all the sober judgment he could muster if he wanted to be alive and still marshal when the sun went down.

Claire came up beside him as he raised the glass and sipped the beer. She said softly, "I'm sorry, Frank."

He turned his head and looked at her. There were times when Claire was positively beautiful, and this was one of them. He said, "So am I, Claire. I liked

Oxley and I've known him a long, long time."

"Why did he do it, Frank? Why?"

"I guess I forced him to. He felt threatened."

"With what? What could you possibly threaten Oxley with?"

"Something that happened a long time ago."

Claire was silent for several moments. Patch gulped his beer and turned to go but Claire reached out and touched his arm. "Let them have the job, Frank. Let them have it back. We can go away. I'll sell out and we can go away. This is a big country, and we could find a ranch someplace. . . ."

He looked down at her. "I'd end up my life milking cows and slopping hogs."

"Frank, there's worse things than that."

He shook his head almost angrily and pulled away from her. He strode to the doors and slammed through them into the street.

He untied the black and led him up the

street to the jail. He tied the horse in front, knowing he might need the black today, might need him quickly and desperately at any time. Patch went inside.

Chester Sayre was sitting in the chair beside his desk, smoking a cigar. He nodded as Patch came in and held out a cigar. "Hello Frank. Have a cigar?"

Patch shook his head. He stood just inside the door, staring across at Sayre. "What do you want?"

"Same thing as before. This can't go on, Frank. First Luke Mills, now Andrew Oxley. Who's going to be next?"

"Nobody if they'll quit trying to put a bullet hole in me."

"But they won't quit, Frank. The town's stirred up. As soon as Will gets over the shock of his father's death, he'll probably try to kill you, too. What will you do when he does? Shoot him the way you shot his father a while ago?"

Patch stared harshly at him. "You sound like you condone murder, Mr. Mayor. You sound like you think it'd be

124

all right for Will to murder me."

Sayre shook his head. "What's happening in this town doesn't need me to approve or disapprove. It's happening, and there's nobody that can stop it but you. Quit, Frank. I'll see to it that you get a pension until you die."

Patch looked at him sourly. "Fifteen or twenty a month. With that I could pay my room at the hotel and eat, if I didn't eat too much. I could even have a beer on Saturday night with what I had left."

"What's so bad about that?"

"Would you settle for it?"

Sayre looked at him exasperatedly. "We're not talking about me. We're talking about you."

"And I've told you how I feel." There was an implacable kind of stubbornness in Frank Patch now. Sayre realized suddenly how stiff that stubbornness had become. Luke Mills's death two weeks ago had begun to stiffen it. The shooting of Oxley a little while ago had further stiffened it. There was very little chance of getting Patch to resign voluntarily. He'd have to be forced to quit.

Sayre got reluctantly to his feet. "I hoped you'd be looking at it differently since Oxley's death. But I guess you're not."

Patch did not reply. Sayre went past him and out the door. He went down the short walk to the sagging fence and out onto the boardwalk before the jail. He turned uptown toward his store.

Arriving, he sent a clerk to the courthouse at the upper end of Elm to get Lou Trinidad.

He waited impatiently, pacing back and forth. The clerk returned with the message that Trinidad would be there right away.

Half a dozen times in the next half hour, Sayre went to the window and stared up Elm. Half a dozen times he cursed sourly to himself. But at last Trinidad opened the door and stepped into the store.

He was a short, stocky man. His dark complexion and straight black hair were bequests from his Spanish ancestors, as

126

was his name. He nodded at Sayre. "Morning, Ches."

Sayre nodded irritably. He said, "Lou, you've got to do something about Patch."

Trinidad stared at him impassively, a little smile touching his mouth. "I've got to do something? Why me? I'm the county sheriff, and this is a town problem, not a county one."

"If a man commits a crime in the county, then it is your problem, Lou."

"Crime? What crime?"

"Patch shot Andrew Oxley this morning. You know that."

Trinidad shook his head. "Oh no you don't. Shooting back at someone who's shooting at you isn't a crime. Not even in this progressive, enlightened community."

Sayre said, "If a citizen swears out a complaint, you've got to act on it. I know that much law."

"Are you going to swear out a complaint?"

Sayre nodded. "If it's the only way to

get you off your butt, I am."

Trinidad flushed angrily. His black eyes snapped. He said, "All right, come on up to the office and sign your goddam complaint. But you're making a mistake. Patch is a damned good man. I'm just glad he never went after my job because he'd have got it sure."

Sayre said stubbornly, "He's a killer. He's too damned good with that gun of his. You can't go around shooting respectable citizens in the street. Not in this day and age."

"I wouldn't say they were so respectable. They were trying to kill him, or they wouldn't have got shot."

Sayre said, "It's gone too far. He's got to get out, that's all. I can't answer for what will happen in this town if he doesn't quit."

Trinidad shrugged, but for all his show of unconcern, there was worry in his eyes. He didn't want to be forced into a showdown with Patch. Not even if he had a score of men to back him up. He knew Patch would never surrender his gun and let himself be put in jail. Trinidad said, "All right, come on."

Sayre followed him out the door and into the street. He hurried along beside Trinidad toward the courthouse at the upper end of the street. He had an overwhelming feeling of depression, as if he had gone past the point of no return.

Lou Trinidad's anger increased with every step he took between Sayre's Dry Goods Store and the courthouse at the upper end of Elm. By the time Trinidad and Sayre reached the bronze statue of General Grant standing in the middle of the courthouse lawn Trinidad was furious.

He slammed open the basement door leading to the county jail and went in, not bothering to look behind to see if Sayre was following. The sheriff slammed up the cover of his roll-top desk with a bang that could have been heard all the way out in the street. He raked out a pile of forms and selected one from the pile. He sat down in the creaking swivel chair and began to fill out the form.

Back in the jail someone started to bang on the bars and yell for him. Trinidad stood the noise for about a minute, then roared, "Shut up, you damn fool, or I'll come back there and break your arm!"

Sayre said, "Whew!"

Trinidad glanced up and scowled at him.

Sayre asked, "Who's that back there?"

"Horse thief. He's waitin' trial." He looked back at the paper on his desk with plain disgust. Finally he stood up, waving his hand at the desk. "The hell with it. You fill it out. You know what you're goin' to charge him with better than I do."

Sayre sat down in the swivel chair and picked up the pen. He scowled at the paper in front of him. Trinidad said irritably, "Go on, go on! You got me up here to file a complaint. Now file the goddam thing."

Sayre glanced up uncertainly. "I can't hardly put down murder on this thing.

He'd get off easy from a charge like that. He can find a dozen men that will swear Oxley fired twice before he even unlimbered his gun."

Trinidad gave him no help. He stared at Sayre with uncompromising disfavor.

Sayre flushed slightly, his neck turning darker than his face. He said lamely, "I could charge him with malfeasance in office. Or with gross misconduct. Or something like that."

Trinidad said sourly, "Or you might charge him with discharging a firearm within the town limits. You've got an ordinance against it, haven't you?"

Sayre nodded, glancing at Trinidad to see what his expression was. He mumbled as he wrote, "That'll do as well as anything."

Trinidad said disgustedly, "Hold it. I can't serve a complaint on Patch for violation of a town ordinance. You'll have to dream up a violation of state law, or I can't do a thing."

Sayre wadded up the paper and threw it on the floor. He thumbed through the pile and came up with a fresh form. Scowling, he said, "All right then, damn it. I'll make it a lunacy complaint. I'll say that he's wandering at large and deemed to be a lunatic. Isn't that the way it's supposed to read?"

Trinidad nodded sourly. "I'll have to sign it, too, and you'll have to have at least one medical certificate."

Sayre scratched in silence for several minutes. When he had finished, Trinidad said, "Sign it at the bottom, Mr. Mayor. Then you can go see if Doc Pugh will certify that Patch is insane. After that, I'll see if I can get a posse up."

"Posse? That'll make more trouble than we've already got."

Trinidad looked at him steadily. "You know Patch, Mr. Sayre. If he doesn't want to accept service of that complaint, he'll tell me what to do with it. And I'll tell you something. I won't force the issue. Not with Patch. I'm not even going to scratch myself while I'm in his office facin' him." He stared at Sayre challengingly. "Still want me to go down

132

there alone?"

Sayre nodded. "Forget the posse, Lou. I'm not going to be responsible for a lot more people getting killed. You go down there alone and see what you can do. He might have enough respect for the law . . ."

Trinidad laughed softly. "He's got respect for the law, Mr. Sayre. He's spent his life upholding it. It's you that's got no respect for it. Or for the promises you made to him twenty years ago."

"I don't have to take that from you."

"Don't you, Mr. Sayre? You might have a lot of political power hereabouts, but my term has still got a year to run. And I'll say what I think."

Sayre glared a moment more. Then, as sulkily as a boy, he turned and shuffled from the office. He clumped up the three stone steps to the level of the lawn, opened the courthouse door and went outside. He kicked savagely at a pile of yellow leaves the wind had blown against the building, scattering them. He glanced up guiltily afterward and looked around to see if anyone had noticed him.

No one had. He stepped out along the gravel walk, down toward Doc Pugh's office over his store. He was beginning to wish they'd never started this. He had an uneasy certainty that the trouble wasn't over with. Not yet. Not by a long shot.

He reached the stairway leading from the boardwalk up to Doc Pugh's office over the dry goods store. He climbed the steps feeling the sun hot against his back. He opened the door and went inside.

Doc Pugh was sitting on his rumpled bed. His eyes were red, his mouth slack. He picked up a bottle from the floor as Sayre came in, pulled the cork and took a drink. The room smelled sour, of whiskey, of bedclothes, of iodoform.

Sayre said, "I want a medical certificate from you saying that Frank Patch is insane."

Doc Pugh looked up at Sayre as if he were the one who was insane. Sayre said irritably, "I've put up with a lot from you and so has the town. You rent this office from me, and you're six months behind in your rent. So don't give me any argument. Just make out a medical certificate saying Patch is insane, and you can drown yourself in that damned bottle for all I care."

Pugh continued to stare at him, something angrily resentful in his eyes. For a moment Sayre thought Pugh was going to refuse, but he did not. He ducked his head, got up off the bed and staggered across the room to his desk. He fumbled interminably before he found a sheet of paper and a pen. He sat down and scratched steadily for several minutes. He got up and handed the paper to Sayre. There was steady hatred in his eyes as he looked at Sayre, but he didn't say a word. Sayre turned and went out. He went down the outside stairway to the walk.

He went back to the courthouse and gave the paper to Lou Trinidad, then retraced his steps to his store once more. He went in, glancing behind at the courthouse as he did. From the shadows

halfway to the rear of his store he saw the sheriff pass. He hurried back to the window so that he could watch.

Chapter 10

Dan Joslyn sat on the steps sobbing for a long, long time. Finally, becoming aware of where he was and afraid he would be seen, he got to his feet and wandered toward the creek.

He went down through the weeds and brush to the creek bank, knelt and splashed water into his face to wash away the traces of his tears. He was ashamed of himself for bawling like that. He hoped nobody had seen. He'd never live it down if they had and if they told on him.

He was too big to be bawling anyway. It was just that seeing Patch kill Mr. Oxley had been too great a shock. He'd never seen anything like it before. He knew people got killed and he'd read about killings and heard them talked about, but that was different from seeing

137

one. There was an awful finality about watching someone killed. One minute the person was standing there, alive, with a character like that of no one else. Then suddenly he was lying in the dirt with blood spreading over him, and you knew he'd never get up again, or breathe, or speak, or eat or sleep. He was suddenly nothing, just a lump of flesh dressed in dusty, bloody clothes.

Dan dried his face with his sleeve. Remembering the scuffed boot, he stuck his fingers in the creek, wet the scuffed place and smoothed it out so that it wouldn't show. He didn't want Patch to see the scuffed place if it could be hidden. He didn't want Patch to think he was careless with the boots or that he didn't value them.

He hesitated there in the creek bottom. Above him the cottonwood leaves, brilliant yellow in the sun, rustled in the breeze. There was a dusty, dry smell about the air, and there was a haze in the distance, almost like smoke lying low above the land.

Dan didn't want to go back to the boardinghouse. He didn't want to talk to anyone, unless it would be Patch. But he was half afraid to go back to the marshal's office at the upper end of Elm.

Dan climbed reluctantly out of the bottom of the creek. He stood there in the weeds, staring at the town he knew so well, staring but suddenly feeling almost like a stranger there. He didn't trust his own feelings, and he didn't trust his judgment any more.

Frowning, he scuffed along through the dust toward Elm. He watched the way dust coated the scuffed place on his boot and was glad it did. He couldn't help the way his thoughts kept wandering back to the reasons Oxley might have had for trying to kill Frank Patch. Dan's mind kept speculating, in spite of his feeling of being disloyal to Patch when he did.

Oxley had been mistaken, he stoutly told himself. Oxley had been wrong. That had to be the answer. That had to be it.

Dan moved on down Texas Street to Elm. As he came into Elm, he heard the noise from the Alamo Saloon, the loud talking and the yells.

He suddenly felt very sorry for Patch. It must be awful to have everyone against you the way they were all against Frank Patch.

Feeling sorry for Patch made Dan less afraid, and he headed for the marshal's office in the jail. He saw Claire Quintana come out of the Goliad and stand there a moment staring upstreet at the jail, shading her eyes against the sun with an upraised hand.

She was an awfully good-looking woman, he thought, in spite of the fact that she was pretty old. She made him feel ... He shook his head impatiently. She was Patch's woman, even though Patch had never married her. Everybody in town knew she belonged to Patch.

Claire went back into the Goliad, and Dan continued toward the jail. He hoped the trouble was over but a strange uneasiness told him it was not. They'd keep on trying to get rid of Patch. And if the marshal continued to refuse to quit . . . Dan's spine felt cold.

He went up the walk to the office and went through the open door. There was the stale smell of cigar smoke in the place, and the smell of Patch's pipe. There was the smell of the disinfectant that was used in the jail cells, and there was the peculiar dusty smell that was always there. Dan didn't know what he was going to say. He looked at Patch and suddenly wanted to cry again.

He bit his lip angrily. Patch said, "Hello Dan."

The marshal's voice was sober, serious. It had a quality Dan had never heard in it before. As though Patch was worried about what the boy thought.

He said, "Hello, Mr. Patch."

Patch turned in the swivel chair so that he was facing Dan. He waited until Dan looked at him before he spoke. "I couldn't help it, Dan. He'd have killed me if I hadn't defended myself."

141

Dan nodded and looked away. "I know that, Mr. Patch."

Patch studied him several moments before he said slowly, "It's hard, seeing your first man killed. One minute he's there, and alive, someone you know maybe and then suddenly he's dead and only a little blood and the smell of powdersmoke to tell what caused his death."

Dan glanced at him gratefully, surprised that Patch understood the way he felt. But Patch wasn't looking at him. He had a faraway look in his eyes, as though he were looking backward down the years at something that had happened a long, long time ago. Almost as though talking to himself, Patch went on, "It's easy to blame someone for the death. It helps. If you can blame someone, it kind of takes away the sting. So you go ahead and blame me, Dan, if it helps the way you feel."

Dan said quickly, "I ain't blaming you. I saw the way it was. But I keep wondering . . ."

"You keep wondering what?"

"Why he did it, Mr. Patch. Mr. Oxley never hurt nobody in his life. Why did he suddenly go get a gun and try to shoot you with it?"

He didn't look at Patch as he spoke. His throat was almost closed with fright at his own temerity. But he had to know. He had to know.

Patch didn't answer him immediately. Dan heard footsteps outside the door and looked up to see the sheriff, Lou Trinidad, coming up the path, a couple of folded papers in his hand.

Trinidad came in. He stopped just inside the door, looked at Patch, then at Dan and then back to Patch. He crossed the room slowly, the papers in his right hand, his left hand held away from his body as if to show how empty it was. He nodded. "Hello, Frank."

"Hello, Lou."

"I have a lunacy complaint, Frank, and a medical certificate. I've got to take you into custody and send you to Osawatomie."

Patch didn't say anything but Dan, who was watching his face, saw the change in it. Patch took the papers from Trinidad, unfolded them and stared down at them. His lips moved as he read the words laboriously. When he had finished reading the complaint, he read Doc Pugh's certificate. His eyes were bitter as he looked up at Trinidad. "You know this is a bunch of lies. You know there's nothing wrong with me, and so does everybody else. This is a cheap trick, and you're letting yourself be made a part of it."

Trinidad couldn't meet his eyes.

Patch said, "They know they can't make this stick but they don't even expect to make it stick. They just want me out of the way for a while. By the time I get back, there'll be somebody else in my job."

Dan glanced from Patch's face to Trinidad's and back again. Patch was thoroughly angry now, and it was one of the very few times Dan had seen him so. His face had turned a dark shade of red, and his eyes had narrowed until they were only slits. His mouth was a slash, and a network of veins stood out on his forehead and in his neck. Glancing down at the complaint and certificate, he deliberately ripped them in two, then ripped them again, and again, until the pieces were too small to tear. He threw the handful of scraps disgustedly at the spittoon. "That's what I think of your goddam commitment papers, Lou." He spat at the spittoon. "And that's what I think of you. Now if you think you can take me, go ahead."

Trinidad's face had lost what color it possessed. It was almost gray. His voice was weak and thin as he said, "When a citizen wants me to file a complaint, I have no choice. That's my job."

Patch uttered a contemptuous obscenity. He stood there, motionless but loose and relaxed, staring steadily at Trinidad.

Trinidad's body tensed. His right hand became like a claw. Dan knew that in a minute he was going to grab his gun, and then Patch's gun would roar and Trinidad would be as dead as Mr. Oxley was.

But Trinidad didn't draw his gun. His face began to sweat until rivulets began to course from his forehead down his cheeks. His eyes had the same look as those of a cornered rabbit.

Patch began to move toward him, a steady step at a time. His voice was savage, soft, contemptuous. "I'm going to take your gun away from you, you damned little greaser rat. I'm going to stuff it down your throat until you gag on it. Then I'm going to kick you clear out into the street so the whole damned county can see what they elected for sheriff when they elected you."

Trinidad took a backward step, another, a third. He reached the door and tried to back out of it.

Patch lunged at him just as he reached the door. Trinidad took too hasty a backward step and tripped on the threshold. He fell out the door and onto the dusty porch.

Instantly, he rolled and tried to scramble to his feet. He was on his hands and knees when Patch reached him and swung his booted foot.

The foot connected squarely with the sheriff's rump, driving him forward, making his face skid along the dirt of the path before he could get his hands under him again.

Patch stood still, then, and let Trinidad get up to his feet. The sheriff whirled furiously. His nose was bleeding, both from the nostrils and from the skinned place on it. His face, which had been so sweaty, was now covered with dust and with mud formed by the combination of sweat and dust. Patch said, "Maybe you're mad enough now, Lou. Maybe you're mad enough."

For a moment, Dan thought the sheriff was going to snatch his gun. But he changed his mind again. He turned his back and shuffled away, his head hanging, digging at his eyes with his knuckles and cursing beneath his breath.

Dan, who had come out the door

behind Patch, said, "You didn't have to do that. You didn't have to make him eat dirt."

Patch whirled. His face was still congested, and his eyes still blazed.

Dan met his glance steadily, although he was trembling inside.

Patch roared, "And I suppose I didn't have to kill Oxley. And I didn't have to kill Luke Mills. What should I have done, you damned smart kid?"

Dan's face turned white. His hands and knees began to shake. He said, "You could act like a marshal's supposed to act, and if you can't do that, you could get out. You done something to Mr. Oxley to make him do what he did. Maybe you done something like you just done to Mr. Trinidad."

"You watch your tongue!"

Dan didn't say anything after that, but his eyes stared defiance at Patch. Suddenly Patch's hand swung out. The flat of it struck Dan on the side of his face.

The blow rocked Dan's head and put a

brassy taste in his mouth. He stared steadily at Patch for a moment longer then turned and ran frantically for the boardinghouse. He was going to cry again, and he was damned if he'd let Patch see him cry.

Patch stared after him. The anger was gone from the marshal's face. His eyes were narrowed down, as though from pain. With his shoulders sagging, he turned and went back inside. He closed the door behind him carefully.

Chapter 11

Dan ran as far as Maple Street and turned the corner out of sight of the jail. He stopped then, furious at himself for crying a second time today. He knuckled his eyes angrily.

For several moments he stood there, confusion in his thoughts. He felt as though the sunlight had gone from the day. He felt as he'd felt that day six years ago when his aunt had died, leaving him alone in the world. He felt alone right now, as though Patch had died, or worse, as though Patch had simply gone off and abandoned him.

He didn't know what to think. Patch had always been like a god to him, someone who could do no wrong. Yet Patch had done wrong today. Despite his claim that the shooting of Oxley had been self-defense, there had been something wrong with the incident. And it had been wrong of Patch to shame Lou Trinidad, even if Trinidad had let himself be part of a shoddy attempt to put Patch away. Dan was old enough to realize that what Patch had done to Trinidad a little while ago would leave scars that might never heal.

Dan passed the alley between Elm and Maple and heard a voice call out to him. "Hey Dan. Where'd you git them fancy boots?"

He turned his head. There were three kids in the alley, Art Early, Fletch Kirby and Ned Olivares. Art was the one who had spoken, a freckled, red-haired boy about two inches taller than Dan.

Dan stopped. "You know where I got 'em." He stood there motionless while the three boys approached. Art stopped in front of him. The other two moved a little to one side.

"Patch give 'em to you?"

Dan felt mean and quarrelsome. He said, "You know damn well he gave 'em to me. You got anything to say about it?"

151

"Maybe. I wouldn't wear boots that was given me by a killer." Art turned his head. "Would you?" he asked the other boys.

Dan felt his knees begin to shake. He wasn't afraid, but he suddenly knew this was going to end in a fight. He started to push on past, but Art's voice stopped him a second time. "Hey! You been bawlin', Dan?" He turned his head again. "Look at him! He's been bawlin' like a goddam girl!"

Dan's anger was instantaneous. And he acted instantaneously. He swung a haymaker at Art, a blow that connected with the side of Art's head just below his ear.

Art was flung aside by the force of the blow and fell in the alley dirt. The other two boys stared at Dan in amazement for an instant, then at Art lying on the ground. Art got up. There was a trickle of blood coming from his ear. He swiped at it, looked at his hand, then glared at Dan. "You crazy fool! I'll beat the stuffin's out of you for that!"

Dan waited. Art launched himself at Dan, to be met by another wild swing. This one missed.

He closed with Dan, and they wrestled briefly, finally falling and thereafter wrestling on the ground.

Although shorter, Dan was stronger than Art. He got Art down on his back and began pummeling his face. Dan was angry and he still felt mean. The blows seemed to ease some of the hurt in him, some of his disappointment in Patch, some of his disillusionment. He heard someone yelling at him, but he didn't want to stop. Suddenly something struck him on the head, and he felt himself driven sideways, away from Art, whose body he had been straddling.

All three of the boys were after him now, kicking, hitting. He felt himself banged against a building wall and struggled to pull himself erect. A fist smashed him squarely in the mouth. Another struck him in the nose. A third slammed into his ear.

There was blood on his face and dust,

and there was more anger in him than he had ever felt in his life before. He struck out again and again, sometimes hitting his tormentors, sometimes missing them. He began to sob with anger, and tears mingled with the dust and blood on his face.

It was this anger that made Dan's three opponents give up, because they sensed, perhaps, that Dan Joslyn never would. They drew back, leaving him standing in the alley with his back to the building wall. He was cursing them and sobbing almost hysterically between curses. They turned and shuffled away, leaving him with nothing to vent his anger on, with nothing to fight except his own awful feeling of loneliness, his feeling of having been betrayed.

He glared after them until they were out of sight behind a sagging fence. Then, head down, he shuffled toward the boardinghouse. He'd have to sneak into the place if he didn't want a lot of questions asked.

Staring down at his feet, he saw that

the boots were badly scuffed from the fight. He stopped, knelt and tried to brush them off with one hand.

He felt tears burning behind his eyes again, tears of frustration and disappointment. He'd wanted to keep these boots bright and shining and new, and now they were scuffed and dirty and could never be that way again. He felt like taking them off and throwing them away. He resisted the impulse and went on toward the boardinghouse. The boots still covered his feet and were still something to be proud of even if they weren't perfect any more.

He came up the alley behind the boardinghouse, skulking along now because he did not want to be seen. But as he came through the back gate and headed for the pump, he heard Hilda say, "Dan! What in the world . . .?"

He scowled at her. She was hanging clothes on the line and talking with two clothespins stuck in her mouth.

He turned to face her as she insisted, "Dan!" and growled, "Why don't you mind your own damn business anyway? I been in a fight. Any fool could see that, even you."

She flinched as though he had struck her. He was sorry instantly for what he'd said. But he couldn't take it back. He couldn't, not the way he was feeling now.

What was the matter with him anyway? He'd cried like a baby today and felt like crying again, and he was almost sixteen years old. Angrily he stamped across the yard to the pump and angrily worked the handle until water came gushing out. He stuck his head under the icy stream, then his hands, and afterward scrubbed vigorously in spite of the way the lacerations burned and stung. He reached for the towel that hung from a nail on the washstand nearby.

He dried his face and hands, picked up the broken comb that was always on the washstand and ran it through his hair.

Hilda had finished hanging up the clothes and now picked up the basket and carried it toward the house. As she passed him, she said in a subdued voice, "Ma said the woodbox is almost empty, Dan."

"All right. I'll fill it up." He let her go by and then said hesitantly, "Hilda?"

She turned eagerly.

"I . . . I didn't mean . . ."

She interrupted anxiously, "It's all right Dan. I had no right to be so nosy."

He said, "The fight was about the boots. And about Mr. Patch, I guess."

Hilda nodded. There was something agonizing in her eyes as she looked so steadily at him, as though she knew . . . about his uncertainty and confusion. He felt his eyes begin to burn. "I'll get the wood," he said, and bolted for the woodshed. Hilda stood looking after him for a moment. Then she took the basket into the house.

Upon hearing the shots in the street, Lester Locke hurried to the swinging doors of the Alamo. He saw Patch's nervously dancing horse up in front of the sandstone jail. He saw Patch rolling in the dust. He also saw the bluish powdersmoke drifting out from the passageway between the two-story warehouse and the building next to it.

It took an instant before he realized what was happening. Someone was trying to kill Frank Patch! Someone had mustered the nerve to cut loose on him from that passageway!

The instant Locke realized this he whirled and ran behind the bar. He knocked over half a dozen bottles in his haste, and one of them broke in the fall. Ignoring that, he snatched the shotgun from beneath the bar and hurried to the doors again.

He arrived just as Oxley and Patch fired simultaneously, and Locke saw Oxley fall. Patch remained on his feet. Patch had not been hit.

Locke's shotgun was pointed toward the marshal, but the range was too great for any certainty. One of the buckshot in the gun might happen to strike Patch in a vital spot. It also might not. And Locke didn't feel like taking that kind of chance. Not with Patch.

He muttered an angry, bitter curse. If he'd only known Oxley was going to ambush Patch, he could have been waiting here with a rifle, and he wouldn't have missed the way Oxley had. No one would have been any wiser, either. The townspeople would have thought one of Oxley's bullets had killed Patch. They wouldn't have known Locke had had anything to do with Patch's death.

Disgustedly, Locke carried the shotgun back behind the bar and replaced it in its customary place. He returned to the swinging doors to watch what was happening.

Patch was kneeling at Oxley's side. He seemed to be talking to Oxley but at this distance Locke could not be sure. At last Patch got up. The marshal stared down at Oxley's body for several moments then turned to stare at the townsmen, approaching from uptown.

Angrily, then, Patch turned and stalked to his horse. He mounted, whirled the horse and spurred away toward the lower end of town. Locke got a good look at the marshal's face as he passed the Alamo, riding as though he was pursued. The look on Patch's face made a little spot of coldness grow in Locke's spine.

In front of the jail the townsmen were gathering, forming a ring around Oxley's body on the ground. Locke went out and walked slowly along the boardwalk toward the group. He didn't intend to volunteer any testimony as to how the killing had happened. He didn't want to help Patch by clearing him, but neither did he want to say Patch had not acted in self-defense. Locke wanted to remain inconspicuous as far as Patch was concerned. He didn't even want Patch to notice him. He might get a chance at Patch later on. He didn't intend to have that chance spoiled because the marshal was watching him.

Generally, the mood of the townsmen was one of outrage and unbelief. All of them had known Andrew Oxley, and none could believe he had done what it appeared certain he had done. It seemed incredible that Oxley should try to murder Patch.

One man asked of the crowd at large, "Why'd he do it? Why? What possible reason could Oxley have for killing Patch?"

Nobody answered him. Some of them lifted Oxley's body and began to carry it toward his house. Will, still wearing his printer's apron, came from the newspaper office and walked in stunned silence behind those who were carrying his father's body home.

Locke watched the boy interestedly. The bartender had not been able to help Oxley get rid of Patch for the simple reason he hadn't known Oxley intended to get rid of him.

Locke wouldn't make the same mistake again. Maybe Will Oxley wasn't thinking in terms of avenging his father yet. But the boy would, later on. When the shock wore off, he'd be wanting his revenge.

When Will began to feel that way,

Locke intended to be close at hand. His hard mouth curved into a small, humorless smile. Will couldn't kill Patch by himself. But with a little help, Will could and would. And Locke would still be in the clear, if he worked things right.

He turned and walked back to the Alamo. There were already half a dozen men at the bar, waiting to be served.

Locke drew beer, poured whiskey, and replenished the food on the free lunch counter. He listened silently to the talk.

Feeling was running high against Patch right now. It would go on running high all day. By nightfall, or sooner, the town might be ready to accept Patch's death without wanting to punish his murderer. And if Patch was killed by Will Oxley today . . . hell, there weren't twelve men in the county that would adjudge Will guilty of anything but justifiable homicide.

Excitement was stirring in Locke. His eyes gleamed with it. His mouth wore a tight, small smile. With a little luck he'd get that goddamned Patch today. He'd get him once and for all, and that would be an end to it.

Chapter 12

Frank Patch stood for several moments with his back to the door. The palm of his hand still stung from the blow he had struck against the side of Dan Joslyn's face.

When he did move, he discovered that both fists were clenched. His stomach felt hollow. There was a leaden feeling in his mind and heart. He wished desperately that he could recall the blow, that he could recall the words that had preceded it.

But he could not. The only alternative was apology. He could apologize to Dan, and would, the first time he saw the boy.

In the meantime Patch began to pace back and forth across the office floor in the nervous, light-footed way of a caged mountain lion. In the meantime he'd feel like a dog for having struck Dan the way he had, and he'd feel ashamed of the things he'd said.

And he'd know, whether he liked admitting it or not, that young Dan had been right. Patch had forced Oxley to try killing him. He had been arrogant and brutal with Lou Trinidad and had humiliated him unnecessarily.

But Trinidad had been humiliated and had been forced to admit a truth about himself . . . that he had not the courage necessary to continue in the sheriff's job. Trinidad had been deluding himself successfully for years, but now he could delude himself no more. He would have to quit. Patch, in trying to defend his own right to his job, had destroyed Trinidad's chance to continue holding the sheriff's job.

Patch strode to the window and stared, scowling, into the street. What was happening to him? What was changing him? Today he had killed a friend, and the killing had been stupid and reasonless. He had alienated Dan, and he had destroyed Trinidad by destroying the sheriff's necessary illusions about himself. The worst part of all was that Patch hadn't wanted to do any of these things.

Yet in spite of his distaste for himself, in spite of his admission that he had been wrong, a hard core of stubbornness remained in Patch. The more pressure that the townsmen put on him, the more stubbornly he would resist.

He had a right to his job, he repeated to himself irritably, and these people had no right to try to put him out of it. They had promised him that the job was his for as long as he wanted it.

And he still wanted it. He wanted it desperately. He got a nasty chill in his spine when he thought of what it would be like not having this job. He'd be nothing. He'd be like the least of men, less even than Luke Mills had been.

That was something Patch couldn't bear – the thought of being nothing, of being ordinary, even less than ordinary. There'd be no excuse for his continued existence if he gave up this job. He'd be like an old Indian he had come upon once out on the Kansas prairie, an Indian left there to die because he was too old and too senile to continue living with the tribe, left out there alone because it was time for him to die.

The tempo of the marshal's pacing increased. Damn these people. Damn them anyway! It wasn't he who was in the wrong, and he was stupid to let them succeed in making him feel that he was. It was the townsmen that were wrong, Sayre and Stanek and the rest, who had promised him this job and who now wanted to take it away from him.

Well, to hell with them. He wasn't going to give it up. He hadn't done anything he shouldn't have. He'd had a right to defend himself against Luke Mills's gun two weeks ago and he'd had a right to defend himself against Oxley's rifle earlier today.

Patch stopped pacing suddenly. He went to his desk and forced himself to sit down in his creaking swivel chair. He picked up his pipe and tobacco from the desk and deliberately cleaned and refilled the pipe. He lighted it and puffed slowly and deliberately.

He raised one of his hands, fingers spread, and stared at it. There were tremors in that hand, in the stubby, dark-tanned fingers, the backs of which were thickly covered with fine short hair. There were tremors in his fingers that had never been there before.

He thought of Dan, and his face twisted with his thoughts. He forced himself to think of Claire, and a measure of serenity replaced the pain.

Two people, he thought. Two people of all those in Cottonwood Springs. He was close to only two. Suddenly he wanted to see Claire.

He crossed to the door and opened it. He stared out into the street. From here he could see the passageway where Oxley had hidden himself. Patch could see the spot where Oxley had fallen and the scuffed marks in the dust made by himself and by the men who had lifted

Oxley's body and carried it away toward home.

How many more, he wondered bleakly. How many more would he have to kill before it stopped? Will Oxley? Would Will think he owed it to his father to avenge him? Patch would have to kill Will, too, unless the marshal could manage to disarm the boy when the time came. And Will was only a couple of years older than Dan. Patch had watched Will grow from a two-year-old orphan to the eighteen-year-old he was now, a hard-working, quiet young man who was liked and respected by everyone in town.

Patch's face twisted suddenly. Then, with his mouth firm and his eyes narrow, he stepped out and pulled the door shut behind him. He went down the path to the boardwalk beyond the weathered fence and turned toward the Goliad.

At this moment, for the first time in twenty years, Patch was not concerned with his own safety, with protecting himself. Right now he just didn't care.

169

Anyone could have shot him now.

But he could feel the townspeople watching him, and he could feel the hostility of their eyes. As he passed the Drovers Saloon, a man stepped through the doors, saw him and hastily backed into the saloon again.

The action shocked Patch more than anything had thus far. It shocked him to realize that the people of Cottonwood Springs were afraid of him. They were afraid, as though he were a mad dog that would lash out at anyone who dared come near him.

He went on, hearing the buzz of talk inside the Drovers increase. He approached the Alamo.

Two men were standing in front of the Alamo. They had been talking, but now their talking stopped. Patch almost spoke to them, then changed his mind when he saw that neither intended to look at him. He passed them in silence, glaring, wanting to seize the two of them and make them look at him. But he didn't stop. He said nothing, and he

170

didn't touch either of them. He realized that anything he did would only make the situation worse.

He reached the Goliad and went inside. It was cool after the heat in the sun-washed street. It was cool, and it seemed dark. He realized the instant he entered that the place was empty except for Claire Quintana and her bartender, Jake.

Patch walked to the bar. He pushed the hat back on his head and wiped away the thin film of sweat with his hand. He looked aside at Claire, grinning ruefully. "It doesn't pay to know me today."

Claire did not reply. He could feel her glance resting on his face. Jake asked, "What'll it be, Mr. Patch?"

He looked up. "Beer, Jake. And rake off the head."

Jake drew a beer and raked off the head with a stick. He slid the brimming glass along the bar. The glass stopped in front of Patch, who reached out and picked it up. He took a long drink, then wiped his mouth with the back of his hand. He turned and glanced at Claire.

She was watching him with a strange, unreadable expression in her eyes. He tried to fathom that expression, to understand it, but he could not. He looked back at the glass of beer.

Claire asked softly, "How are things going, Frank? Nothing else has happened, has it?" She seemed to be waiting almost breathlessly for his reply.

He said, "Trinidad tried to serve a lunacy complaint on me. I threw him out."

Claire said nothing, and he felt irritability rising in him. He said with angry defiance, "I slapped Dan, too, and gave him hell."

She was still silent when he turned to look at her. All the anger and frustration he was feeling must have been in his eyes and face because she seemed to shrink from him as though she was afraid. He said angrily, "All right, give me hell! I guess I deserve it, so get it over with!"

She regained her composure and said,

"I wasn't going to give you hell. Why would I give you hell? For killing Andrew Oxley? If you hadn't, you wouldn't be standing here. For throwing Lou Trinidad out of your office? He knew he was wrong trying to serve a thing like that on you. He deserved just what he got."

"Then give me hell for slapping Dan. I've been giving myself hell for that."

She smiled. "Dan will get over it. He'll understand."

Patch scowled at his half-empty glass. "He'll do better than I can, then. I'll be damned if I can understand. What's gone wrong with this town, Claire? What's gone wrong with me? I feel like the same man I've always been. This is the same town filled with the same people that have always been here. But something's changed. Something deadly is going on."

She did not reply, and he turned his head and glanced at her. There was stubbornness in his eyes, and her lips were firm with that same stubbornness.

173

She said, "I've told you what I think, and you don't agree with me. I'm not going to nag and I'm not going to keep telling you."

"You think I ought to quit."

"I can't see why you won't. There's nothing here for you any more. You'll never live down Luke Mills and you'll never live Andrew Oxley down. I don't care if you keep trying a thousand years."

Patch picked up his beer and finished it. He put the glass down quietly with controlled fury. He said softly, speaking directly at the glass, "I won't quit. Damn it, I won't quit. I don't care what they do, they're not going to make me quit!"

Claire asked softly, "Why did you come here, Frank? Did you want my advice? Did you want to hear me tell you that you were right? Or did you just want sympathy?"

His face lost color. He said in a rigid voice, "I came in here for a beer. For a beer. That's all."

Claire's voice was equally rigid.

174

"You've finished your beer, and it's on the house. You can leave here at any time."

His fist slammed down furiously on the bar. The empty beer glass jumped. Jake whirled, dropping the glass he had been polishing.

Claire started violently as Patch's fist came down. Now her face was white, her eyes blazing furiously.

Patch turned his head and stared at her. Their glances locked, and held.

Slowly, slowly the rigidness went out of Patch. Slowly his ponderous shoulders slumped. His eyes dropped away from hers. He said softly and reluctantly, "I'm sorry, Claire. I'm sorry. I seem to be doing everything wrong today."

Her face stayed rigid for a long, long time. But at last it began to relax, too. She put out a hand and laid it on Patch's hard, calloused one. She said, "I'm sorry, too. I'm not helping you very much, am I?"

Patch raised his eyes to hers. He made

a short, spare smile. "Nobody can help me much today. I guess that's the fact I have to face. It's all going to be up to me."

Claire said, "You've managed to handle everything that came up in Cottonwood Springs for twenty years. I see no reason to believe you can't do it now."

Patch smiled again. He said, "I guess that's what I really wanted you to say. I guess it's the most anyone can say."

Claire's smile remained steadfast. Patch smiled back at her. He pushed himself away from the bar, leaned close and kissed her lightly on the mouth. Then he headed solidly for the door, a measure of his confidence restored. Behind him tears filled Claire's eyes and spilled down across her cheeks.

Chapter 13

Claire kept her face turned away from Jake. She reached for a small lace handkerchief and dried her tears. Turning, she smiled, her eyes still suspiciously bright and said, "Damn him, Jake, why does he have to be so stubborn? Why can't he give up?"

"It ain't his nature to give up, Miss Claire. That's what makes him what he is. He wouldn't be Frank Patch if he gave up."

She nodded reluctantly. She crossed to the doors, pushed through them and stood just outside in the bright sunlight, staring at the marshal's retreating back.

He was a giant, she thought, an indestructible, fearless giant of a man. For an instant she almost convinced herself that the man didn't live that could kill Frank Patch. When she thought of all the incredible things he had survived. . . .

But he was no giant and he was not indestructible. He was only a man, even though an extraordinary man. He could be killed; he would be killed today, if the townspeople had their way.

An anachronism, they said. Her eyes blazed suddenly. He stood in the way of progress and growth, they said. Her anger flared. But it was helpless anger, just as Patch's anger was. There was nothing she could do, and there was nothing Patch could do. The town had its mind made up. Claire wasn't going to change their decision, and neither was Frank Patch.

Patch disappeared into the jail. Claire turned and re-entered the Goliad. Jake said, "There hasn't been a man in here all day. Except for the marshal."

She smiled bitterly. "And there won't be, Jake. There won't be a customer in here until they've disposed of him. And maybe there won't be then. Maybe they'll feel too guilty about it to come

178

in here."

"You think they'd really try to murder him?"

Claire said softly, "Two of them have already tried."

"Yeah, but they were . . ." Jake left the sentence dangling. He worked behind the bar in silence for several minutes. At last he stopped polishing glasses and looked at her. "What gets into people, anyway? Neither Luke Mills nor Mr. Oxley seemed like the kind to kill anyone."

She shook her head. "I don't know, Jake. I don't know. But it isn't over yet."

She walked to the doors and stepped through them into the street. It was not yet noon, but the sun was almost directly overhead. She raised a hand to shield her eyes from its glare.

Patch's black horse was tied to the rail immediately in front of the jail. He stood with his weight on one rear foot, switching at flies with his tail. Occasionally he would toss his head but never hard enough to tighten up the reins.

179

Claire suddenly felt a coldness in her spine. It was as though she sensed something, as though she knew something terrible would happen to Patch before the day was done. It was as though a premonition told her Patch was going to die.

Pale-faced, cold in spite of the warmth of the noonday sun, she stood there staring at the nearly deserted street. Who would it be that finally killed him, she wondered. Which one of the law-abiding citizens in the town?

Mary Mills worked almost frantically throughout the morning cleaning the house, which had not been touched for more than two weeks. She hung the bedding out to air. She swept and scrubbed. She did a huge washing and hung it on the line.

A film of perspiration formed on her upper lip and dampened both the wisps of hair that had strayed across her forehead and those that had escaped the bun at the back of her neck.

She wasn't sure what time it was when she heard the shots. Sometime in the middle of the morning. She stopped and listened, a frown touching her forehead. Another killing! Had Patch killed someone else?

She went back to her work, but a little later she heard a boy in the alley behind the house. He was shouting excitedly to his mother – Andrew Oxley had been killed by Patch.

Another killing. It seemed unbelievable. Was Patch out of his mind? Oxley had been a respected member of the community for as long as she could remember. Why in the world would Patch shoot Oxley?

She stopped work, poured herself a cup of coffee and sat down. The work hadn't helped compose her thoughts. She kept remembering all the times she had driven Luke from the house with her nagging tongue, the times she had literally driven him to the saloon.

Her face burned as she remembered some of the cutting things she had said to

181

him. Now Luke was gone, and it was too late to make amends.

For a long time, she sat staring at her empty coffee cup. Why couldn't she stop remembering every cruel thing she had ever said to Luke? How long would it be before this awful feeling of guilt went away? And why should she have to feel guilty anyway? Patch was the one who had killed Luke. Patch had shot Andrew Oxley, too.

She discovered that blaming the marshal made it possible for her to stop blaming herself so much. But she also discovered that the more she blamed the marshal, the angrier she got.

Nobody had done a thing to him for killing Luke. Everyone had said it was self-defense and that had been the end of that. Not that she was any better. She'd stood across the grave from Patch, and she hadn't said a blessed thing to him.

It was time somebody told Patch what kind of man he was. It was time somebody let him know that this town wasn't going to tolerate the murder of its

182

citizens in the street. He was hired to keep the peace, not to break it. He was hired to enforce the laws, not to break them himself.

Righteous indignation mounted steadily in her. At last, thoroughly angered, she took off her apron and slipped a sweater on. Maybe nobody else in town would tell the marshal what they thought of him. Maybe the rest of them were afraid. But she certainly was not.

The air was clear, windy, and had that indefinable smell peculiar to fall when the leaves are turning yellow, when the prairie grass is dry. There was a hint of woodsmoke in the breeze, and the sky was dotted with puffy clouds.

She reached Elm Street and turned into it, heading downtown toward the jail. She passed the hotel, her eyes going to the exact spot where Luke had died. The blood spot that had been there at first was gone, but she knew the place anyway. She'd never forget it, not if they paved over it with cobblestones, not if they put a building over it.

Patch's horse was tied before the jail. Mary Mills went through the gate and up the worn and narrow path to the door of Patch's office.

She opened it and stepped inside. Patch, who had been sitting in his swivel chair with his feet up on the desk, turned his head and immediately lowered his feet to the floor. He got up hastily, snatching the hat off his graying head. He said, "Mrs. Mills! What brings you down here, ma'am?"

She stared at him furiously. "You didn't have to kill Luke! You've disarmed men more dangerous than Luke! You killed him because you wanted to!"

Patch said evenly, "You know that isn't true, Mrs. Mills."

"I know nothing of the sort! And what about Mr. Oxley? I suppose you had to kill him too!"

"As a matter of fact I did. He shot at me."

"Who's going to be next? Maybe you'd like to tell me that!"

"I hope nobody, ma'am."

She glared at him. She was just inside the door. On her left was a rack of guns. Patch stood fifteen feet awat, beside his desk.

He looked so calm, so sure, so all-fired sure! Suddenly her hatred for him was overpowering.

Turning, she seized a gun from the rack at her side. She was not familiar with guns and would rather have had a broom or something similar with which she could belabor him. But she knew the gun in her hands was a shotgun because Luke had once owned one similar to it. It had a hammer that had to be pulled back before the gun would shoot. She pulled the hammer back with her thumb and curled her finger through the trigger-guard.

Patch had stiffened when she seized the gun, but otherwise he hadn't moved. All she had to do now was squeeze the trigger a little, she told herself. She'd give Patch what he'd given Luke, and it would serve him right.

Patch didn't say a word. He stared at her, no fear showing in his eyes, only a caution, the kind of caution with which a man will handle dynamite. He seemed to know that any sudden movement, any sudden speech might trigger the gun automatically.

She was close enough to see the pores in his dark-tanned face. She was close enough to see the short gray stubble of whiskers that had sprouted on his face since he'd shaved early that morning in his hotel room. She was close enough to see his eyes, which were hard and competent and sure but which were neither evil nor cruel.

She said shrilly, "I'm doing this because of Luke!"

Patch nodded gravely. "I know, ma'am."

She stared at him unbelievingly. "Aren't you afraid?"

He shook his head.

Her voice rose hysterically. "You don't think I'll do it! You don't think I have the courage for it!"

186

Patch did not answer her, but she could see in his face that he did believe her capable of shooting him. Yet he did not seem to be afraid.

She repeated, "You didn't have to kill him! You could have taken his gun away from him without killing him!"

Patch did not reply.

Mary screamed, "Couldn't you?"

There was a tortured expression on Patch's face. "Ma'am, I don't know. I've asked myself the same question a thousand times, and I still don't know."

The same torment that she was feeling in her heart showed in his eyes, the same guilt that nothing could ever completely wash away. Suddenly she knew she could not kill Patch. She let the gun sag until its muzzle pointed to the floor.

Patch stepped forward and gently took it from her hand. He eased the hammer down, and a long, slow sigh escaped his lips. Then his arm was around her, and he was guiding her toward the door. He said softly, "I'll see you home, Mrs. Mills."

Chapter 14

Patch left Mary Mills at her door and turned back toward the center of town. He walked slowly, his head down, for the first time oblivious of both his surroundings and any danger that might threaten him. He was thinking that he had never been closer to death in his entire life than he had a few minutes before when Mary Mills stood there trembling, pointing that cocked and loaded shotgun at him. She had not fired the gun and afterward had probably convinced herself that she couldn't have fired it. But Patch knew that wasn't true. Any sudden move could have made her fire, any sudden noise outside, any sudden words he himself might have said or movement he might have made.

There were tremors in his body now that the confrontation was over, now that the danger was completely past. He grinned wryly to himself. He must be getting old. Or perhaps he just hadn't had so many close calls in recent years. He wasn't used to them.

Well, he'd better start getting used to them. In two weeks there had been three attempts to take his life.

He reached the office and went in. He closed the door, sat down in his swivel chair, pushed his hat back on his head and put his feet up on the desk. He reached for his pipe and filled it deliberately. He lighted it, filling the room with blue, fragrant clouds of smoke.

Something was stirring in him that had never been there before, something strange and difficult to understand. It was uneasiness; it was premonition. He'd had his hunches through the years and had lived by them, but this was different. This was a cold, icy feeling in his spine; this was a hand squeezing down on his strongly beating heart. This was the face of death, leering from the shadows, grinning death's ugly, fleshless grin. Patch knew there could be no escape today. When nightfall came, he would be dead.

He frowned, wondering why he was so sure. And suddenly he found himself thinking of the past, and remembering.

He remembered Cottonwood Springs when he first had come there, composed of a single, dusty street that turned into a sea of mud in winter or in the rain. He remembered the cheap, false-fronted store buildings here on Elm, when the only really solid building in town had been the jail. Most of those other buildings had been burned in the disastrous fire of '71 and had been replaced by more permanent structures, but he still remembered the old buildings because they were typical of the town and of its attitude during the first few years of its life.

It was a boom town then, here for one reason and only one – to provide a meeting place for cattle drovers and cattle buyers, to provide a shipping point for the endless herds streaming north from the hot lands of Texas into Kansas.

A cattle drive was a three-month affair, and it was natural that the drovers would be hungry for women, hungry for liquor, hungry for release from the pent-up tensions of the drive. But that wasn't all. The drovers were Texas men, men from the defeated South. They were still smarting under that defeat. They hated Yankees, and there were nothing but Yankees in Cottonwood Springs when the drovers arrived. As long as they stayed sober, they could keep their hatred under tight control. But let them get a few drinks in them, and their hostility came boiling out.

Patch had killed five men in the first short week. Five men, and he could still remember every one of them. Not their names. Their faces. Their eyes. Their ages. One of them couldn't have been more than sixteen years old. The age of young Dan. The age Dan would be in a week.

Patch's face softened slightly as he

thought of Dan. Times had changed, and he was glad they had. A boy didn't have to be a man so soon nowadays. Dan wouldn't have to be a man for several years.

Patch had no apologies to make for the things he'd done, for the men he'd killed, for the few he'd crippled but hadn't killed. He was a lawman, and his duty had been to uphold the law. The ones he ran afoul of had been intent on breaking the law or had already broken it.

He had no apologies, but he suddenly found himself counting the dead in his mind. He'd killed three before he ever saw the town of Cottonwood Springs, the first when he was scarcely older than Dan was now. The man had stolen his horse and was riding away on it. Patch got a bead on his back and knocked him out of the saddle with an old smooth-bore rifle that loaded from the muzzle and had a percussion cap in the breech, a converted flintlock made in Kentucky long before Patch was born.

The second man he killed in Wichita when he was thirty. The third, who had come to avenge the second, Patch shot a month later. Both of these men he shot with his revolver, outdrawing them. Both were hit squarely in the heart.

The two killings were his recommendation for the marshal's star in Cottonwood Springs. After the first week, however, Patch didn't need any additional references.

Five dead during his first week as marshal. Three more in the intervening years. And Luke Mills. And Andrew Oxley today. Thirteen men in all, thirteen even, if he weren't forced to kill more before they gave up trying to make him quit his job.

Thirteen were a lot for one man to have killed. Patch had always told himself each killing was justified, but now he began to wonder if he was not deluding himself. Maybe he was just a paid killer for the town, and maybe there was no morality in what he had done. Maybe that was what was troubling the townspeople now. Perhaps they'd like to forget and knew they couldn't forget until they were rid of him.

In more detail, he went over in his mind the men he'd killed one by one, frowning as he did. The first was the only one of the thirteen that hadn't actually threatened his life. In twelve of thirteen cases he had acted in self-defense.

But would his life have been threatened if he hadn't been marshal here? He shook his head reluctantly, admitting it would not have been.

He had killed for the town, then, and for the people that lived in it. A man ought to get appreciation and respect for that. Instead the townspeople only wanted to be rid of him.

By its very nature his job had been a lonely one. He had acquaintances, lots of them, but he had no friends. He had only Claire and Dan. Maybe now he didn't even have Dan. The boy might not want any more to do with him after that slapping episode. Claire, then. Claire was probably all that Patch had left.

He got up and began to pace nervously back and forth, puffing furiously on his pipe. He felt guilty about Claire. He had taken a great deal from her, it seemed to him, giving very little in return.

He stopped pacing long enough to knock the ash out of his pipe and fill it again. He lighted it and resumed his pacing, puffing furiously again.

Once more the cold feeling of premonition touched his mind. He had eleven hundred dollars in the bank, but he had no will. If he was killed today . . .

He'd like Claire to have part of the money, however much as she wanted or needed of it. He would also like for Dan to have some of it. He could make a will, Patch supposed, but wills have to be witnessed, and he didn't want anyone in town to know he had any doubts. If he made out a will, the townspeople would know they had him scared.

Frowning, he paced ever faster back and forth. There was a way, and it was, perhaps, the only way. He could marry

195

Claire. Then she would inherit whatever he had if he died today. And Claire would take care of Dan.

Patch stopped pacing suddenly. He walked to the window and stared into the street. Then, making up his mind, he straightened his hat and went out, knocking the bowl of his pipe against the heel of his hand and emptying the loosened ashes before he reached the walk.

Wary again, he stared up and down the street. He lifted his eyes to the roof of the warehouse across the street. Fleetingly his glance swept along the row of dirty second-story windows and brushed the mouth of the passageway from which Oxley had shot at him earlier. Satisfied, Patch turned down-street toward the Goliad.

There was nervousness in him now, and something that almost felt like fear. He could have faced half a dozen men without feeling this way, but the thought of facing Claire and asking her to marry him . . . He grinned wryly to himself.

There were, perhaps, a score of people on the street. None spoke to him although he passed several close enough to speak. None looked directly at him, instead averting their eyes when he glanced at them. His wry grin of self-derision changed to a tight look of anger and resentment. It made a man mad to be treated like this, particularly when his only crime was doing his job the best he knew how and defending himself against those who would gun him down.

The boardwalk resounded hollowly beneath his feet. It was worn in places. In a few spots there were broken boards. If the people of Cottonwood Springs wanted progress so damned bad, why didn't they start with these outdated walks? In Wichita they had concrete walks. They had cobblestones in the street. It was time the people here started thinking of that kind of improvement for this town, too.

He reached the Goliad and stopped just outside the door. His throat felt dry. He squared his shoulders unconsciously and stepped inside.

Claire was sitting at a table by the window. The table was littered with papers, and there was an account book in front of her. She looked up at him, surprised.

He crossed to the bar, nodding shortly at her. He started to order a drink from Jake, then shook his head instead. He turned and crossed to the table where Claire sat. He stood looking down at her, throat dry, an almost unbearable tension in him.

She stared up at him questioningly, fear growing suddenly in her eyes. "What's the matter? Frank, what's happened? I didn't hear..."

He shook his head, managing a thin-lipped smile. "Nothing's happened, Claire. I came down here to ask you to marry me."

She stared at him unbelievingly, frozen and motionless. The silence ran on and on for what seemed an interminable time. At last Patch growled, "Well, what's so damned strange about

198

that? People do it all the time."

Claire smiled faintly. Her face was paler than he had ever seen it before. She said almost inaudibly, "Sit down, Frank."

He sat across from her, turning the chair and straddling it, resting his arms upon its back. A stiff kind of pride came into his face. He stared at her challengingly, now suddenly afraid she was going to refuse.

She saw the expression and apparently understood it perfectly. She said, "Yes, Frank."

He looked at her unbelievingly. Claire smiled. "I said yes, Frank. You meant what you said when you asked me, didn't you?"

He got up clumsily, knocking over the chair as he did. He went around the table to her, and she helped him by getting to her feet. He put out his arms and drew her close to him.

It was not the first time he had held her. He had held her through many nights over the past five years. But there was a different quality about his embrace today. There was more gentleness than there ever had been in him before. There was awe that was as close to tenderness as Patch would ever come.

Claire felt tears burning in her eyes. She felt her throat close up. And suddenly she was sobbing almost uncontrollably.

She buried her face in Patch's chest. She held on with both her arms tight around his waist. She knew she couldn't look at him right now. She couldn't look at him and still go through with marrying him.

There was no telling what she'd do if she didn't have a moment to compose herself. She might slap his face. She might throw something at him. She might even curse him, for all she knew.

Damn men anyway! Damn Patch in particular! She hadn't expected him to marry her. She was no child. She was an adult woman who could take care of herself.

But he thought he was going to die

today; that was why he had come here. That was why he had asked her to marry him. He thought he was going to die.

And what did he think he could give her by marrying her? His estate? The accumulation of his twenty years as marshal of Cottonwood Springs? Did he think he could give her respectability along with the wedding ring. Damn him! Damn him anyway!

Desperately she fought to control herself. She loosened her clasp around his waist and looked up at him, her eyes swimming with tears. She said, "Yes, Frank. You knew I'd say yes, didn't you?"

"I hoped you would." He sounded uncertain and upset.

She asked, "When, Frank? What day did you have in mind?"

He hesitated a fraction of a second before he said, "Today. Right now. I want you to marry me right now."

She had expected that answer, but it startled her anyway. She clenched her hands into fists, overpoweringly angry at him, yet understanding, too, hurting inside for him because she suddenly believed that he was right. He would die today at the hands of this hostile town. He would die unless she could persuade him to quit.

Briefly she considered making her acceptance a condition to his quitting the marshal's job, but she discarded the idea immediately. Patch would reject such a condition. He'd turn and walk out of the Goliad and out of her life. She said softly, "Give me half an hour, Frank."

He lowered his head and kissed her on the mouth and again, as always in the past, she felt her blood pound hard and fast, felt her head grow light. She pushed him away. "Come back for me in half an hour, Frank."

He stared at her quizzically, as though trying to understand what was going on in her thoughts. Then he turned and stepped outside into the blazing, sun-washed street.

Claire looked at Jake. Tears stood in her eyes, brimming over and running across her cheeks. She choked, "The damned big ox! Does he think a woman like me gets married every day?"

Jake's eyes were filled with understanding. "Only the second time, isn't it Miss Claire?"

She nodded, unable to speak. She turned and, lifting the hem of her skirt, ran upstairs.

She was ready when Patch came back for her. She was ready, dressed in a brown silk dress she had bought in Wichita a month ago. She took his arm and went through the door with him and walked along Texas Street to Oak and up Oak to the parsonage next to the white, tall-steepled Methodist Church.

Patch had apparently spoken to James Rork, the minister, because Rork was waiting for them at the door of the parsonage, a somewhat doubtful smile of welcome on his face.

Claire went into the parlor of the parsonage where Mrs. Rork and her next-door neighbor, Mrs. Stanton, waited to serve as witnesses. The smiles of both were forced.

Patch had put on a fresh shirt and tie and his Sunday suit. He still wore his gun. It seemed almost a blasphemy here, but he didn't offer to take it off.

Holding Claire's hand, he stood before the minister while the words were said. "Dearly beloved, we are gathered here in the sight of God to join this man and this woman in Holy Matrimony. . . . Frank, do you take Claire . . . Claire, do you take Frank, to have and to hold, in sickness and in health, until death do you part?"

Claire nodded. The words, "I do," came out choked from between her nearly colorless lips. The words, "until death do you part," kept ringing in her ears, as though the minister was repeating them over and over again.

She only half heard his final words, "I now pronounce you man and wife." But then Patch's hands were on her shoulders, and he was turning her. He was lowering his head for her kiss.

The minister's wife and her neighbor

left hurriedly. Patch guided Claire toward the door and out into the sun. They began to walk back toward Elm. Claire knew she ought to be happy. All brides were supposed to be that. But all she wanted to do was weep. She only wanted to be alone so that she could weep.

Chapter 15

There were people in the parlor of the Oxley home. There were the muted voices of women mostly, but Will could faintly hear an occasional man's voice too.

The downstairs guest bedroom door was closed. Will sat in a chair beside the bed. His father's body lay there on the bed, his face like wax. A blanket had been laid over him, covering his chest and the stain of blood on it, covering his dusty clothes. But he was dead. He was dead. God damn Frank Patch to hell!

Will suddenly doubled forward, burying his face in his hands. His body shook violently. He covered his mouth, trying to keep his sobs from being heard, but he could not entirely suppress the sound of them.

He sat there weeping for a long, long

time but at last he got up, dried his eyes and face with his handkerchief, crossed to the bed and drew the blanket up to cover his father's face.

Almost as though in a daze, he went down the short hall to the parlor. Immediately several women came toward him, hurriedly putting down their teacups, sympathetic words on their lips.

Will smiled wanly at them. He tried to answer their questions, but he wasn't sure all of his answers made sense because some of the women's faces were perplexed.

He talked to them as long as he could, but suddenly he could stand no more of it. He said, "Excuse me . . ." and bolted out the front door, onto the neatly trimmed front lawn.

There were more people there, people who had come to pay their respects, but Will couldn't talk to them. He ran around the corner of the house toward the woodshed at the rear.

Hidden behind the woodshed, he bent

double, cramping, retching. He hated his weakness, but he couldn't help himself.

All he could think of, suddenly, was that his father had tried to kill Patch. His father had failed and had been killed himself, but that didn't change a thing. There must have been a compelling reason for Oxley to want to kill Patch. Will didn't know what the reason was. He'd probably never know, and it didn't matter anyway. The reason had been compelling enough for his father. It had to be just as compelling to him.

Even if it wasn't, there was an additional reason for Will to finish what his father had begun. The town expected Will to. Or so he thought. And besides, his own honor demanded that he do so.

He straightened and wiped his mouth on a sleeve. He was sweating heavily and felt cold in spite of the warmth of the midday sun. Shivering, he went in the back door.

The kitchen was full of women, who clucked over him as he rushed through to the hall beyond. He could hear their whispered voices behind him as he bolted up the stairs.

There was a gun in his father's dresser drawer, a little nickel-plated revolver that looked more like a woman's gun than a man's. It was loaded, but to Will's knowledge his father had never fired it. He took it out of the drawer and dropped it into his pocket. If he kept his hands in his pockets, he didn't think anybody would notice the bulge.

He went back down the stairs and rushed through the kitchen to the back door. He heard one woman say, "Is that boy goin' to be sick again?"

He cursed the woman silently. He cursed all of them for clustering around clucking like broody hens when all he wanted was to be let alone. He hurried along the alley in the direction of Texas Street.

He began to think of Patch, visualizing the marshal in his mind. Patch was a giant to Will, almost a god. Patch was like the church, like the courthouse, an institution more than a mortal man.

Will reached Texas Street and turned toward Elm. Coldness began to grow in him. It began with his feet. It crept up his lower legs, into his belly and up his spine. It ran down his arms until his hands were like chunks of ice.

He kept seeing Patch in his mind, but Patch kept growing bigger all the time. Patch's stare was enough to make Will turn to mush, and he knew, suddenly, that even if he mustered the courage to walk into the jail, even if he found what it took to do that, he wouldn't be able to draw the gun and he wouldn't be able to fire it, because drawing the gun would bring Patch's gun out of its holster like a striking snake. It would bring those deadly lead-nosed bullets ripping from the gun muzzle, tearing into his flesh as they'd torn into his father's flesh.

He reached the corner of Texas and Elm street. He stared at the jail. The marshal's big black was tied in front, idly switching at flies with his tail, standing head down, drowsing in the sun.

Maybe if he had a drink, Will thought,

maybe if he had a drink or two, he'd still be able to bring the act off. He took a hand out of his pocket and stared at it. It was shaking violently. He stuffed it hastily into his pocket again, then turned and headed for the Alamo. Reaching it, he pushed through the doors.

He had been here with his father several times. He'd always been served sarsaparilla or water, never anything stronger than that. But today – in view of what had happened – he doubted if Locke, the bartender, would refuse him something stronger if he asked for it. The trick was going to be keeping the drink down. The way Will's stomach was...

There were several men in the Alamo. They looked at him with sympathy in their eyes. His father had been well liked here, he thought. He'd been a respected member of the community.

Will crossed to the bar. "I need something today, Mr. Locke. I need it bad."

"Sure you do, boy. Sure you do." Locke got a bottle of whiskey and poured some into a glass. He filled it with water, stirred it and pushed it toward Will. He said, "I'm sorry about your pa. He was a fine man, boy. A real fine man."

Will picked up the glass and gulped down the drink. It had an unpleasant taste, but it warmed his throat. For several moments he thought it was going to come right back up, embarrassing him in front of everyone, but it did not. Locke said, "Stomach actin' up?"

Will gave him a weak grin. "Yes, sir."

"Well, you kep' that one down. Mebbe you can keep another down." Locke refilled Will's glass, putting a little more whiskey in it this time and a little less water to thin the whiskey out. He said, "Drink this one slow. Just drink it slow."

Will nodded. He picked up the glass and sipped its contents cautiously. The flavor was no longer as unpleasant as it had been at first. The drink warmed his throat more than the first one had. And this one made a warm spot in his stomach.

He began to feel a little less shaky than

he had before. He felt less like being sick.

Locke was asking, "What're you going to do?"

"About what?"

"Why about your pa, son, of course. He's dead, boy, he's dead. The marshal gunned him down."

Will gulped the remaining contents of the glass. He stared at Locke, then glanced around at the other men in the place. All of them were watching him, waiting to see what he was going to say. He swallowed. "I'm goin' to kill him, that's what I'm going to do. I'm going to do him just like he done pa."

Locke nodded sympathetically. "Don't blame you a bit, son. I don't blame you a bit. If Patch had killed my pa, I reckon I'd feel the way you do."

He glanced around at the others. He asked, "Ain't that right?"

One of the men said, "Quit eggin' him on, Locke. What're you trying to do, get him killed too?"

Locke stared coldly at the man. "Patch ain't God, my friend. He can be killed. Maybe that's the way to stop the killin's around here once and for all."

"Better not let Patch hear you say that," the man said.

"I'll let him hear when the time for it comes." Locke stared steadily at the man. "The trouble with you, Henry, is that you've got a yellow streak up your back."

The man turned white. It was an instant before he could speak. When he could, he said, "Goddam you, Locke! I'll . . ."

Another man moved in close to Henry and caught his arm. "Locke's looking for a fight. Don't oblige him, Henry. Don't be a fool."

Henry glared a moment more, then allowed himself to be dragged from the saloon. He didn't want a fight with Locke. He was glad to be given a way out that left him with a little pride. Will stared at Locke, then at Henry's back as the man went through the doors followed by his friend and a couple of the other men. Locke grinned at Will. "Now that we're rid of them, maybe we can get down to business."

Two men were left inside the saloon. One was Phil Miller, who tended bar here when Locke was off. The other was Chris Hogg, who rode for one of the small ranchers north of town. Will began to feel a little uneasy because he sensed what was in Locke's mind. But he didn't leave. Maybe Locke and these other two would help him do what he knew he couldn't do by himself. Maybe they'd help him kill Frank Patch.

Will gulped the rest of the drink. Locke poured more whiskey into the glass. This time he apparently forgot to add water to thin the drink out.

Will raised the glass. He took a gulp, startled at the way the liquor burned, at the awful way it tasted straight. But it slid down, leaving his throat warm, leaving recklessness in his thoughts. He was wondering, suddenly, why he had been so afraid of Patch. These men weren't afraid. They weren't afraid to help.

Will had never liked Locke much, but now suddenly he was seeing the man in a different light. Locke couldn't help the way he looked, and there wasn't anything so awful about running a saloon. Right now Locke was being mighty nice to him. Locke studied Will and asked, "You want some help, boy? You can't do it by yourself, and you know you can't."

Will nodded silently. "I know I can't. But I sure was going to try." This was a lie, and Will knew that the minute he said it, but Locke didn't seem to notice. Neither did the other men.

Locke said, "All right then. We want to do it so none of us gets hurt. When it's over with, we'll let Will here take the credit for it." Locke was silent for a moment, studying the other two. At last he said, "Two of us will get up on the roof of that warehouse across from the jail. Will can bust one of those second floor windows out and shoot from there. I'll be down in the passageway where Will's pa was when he tried

216

killin' Patch."

Nobody spoke. Locke looked at Will, then reached out and took Will's glass from his hand. "That's enough of that for now. You want to be able to shoot."

Will wanted more of the whiskey in the glass, but he didn't say anything. Locke went on, "Will's going to have the shotgun I keep here underneath the bar. I'll load it with buck. He can spray Patch from above. I don't see how he's going to miss."

Miller and Hogg nodded. Hogg was looking a little worried now. Locke said, "Phil, there's a couple of rifles in the back room. You and Chris get up on the roof. Get a bead on Patch the minute he opens the jail door. Shoot as soon as you're sure, but let him get far enough from the door so that he can't duck back inside."

Hogg said worriedly, "What if both of us was to miss?"

"It ain't likely that you will. Not both of you and young Will, too. But if all three of you miss ... well, he's got to come through that passageway to get to the stairway out in back of the warehouse so that he can get upstairs. I'll be waiting in the passageway where Oxley was."

Hogg said, "I . . ."

Locke stared angrily at him. "Damn you Chris, don't you even think of backin' out. Not unless you want me tellin' Jess about . . ."

Chris said surlily, "I didn't say nothin' about backin' out. But I'll tell you one thing, Locke. You start threatening me, and I might take a shot at you instead of one at Patch."

Locke smiled placatingly. "Easy, Chris. No sense you an' me fighting, especially at a time like this. You help me out on this, and I'll help you out sometime when you need a hand."

Chris didn't speak after that. Will looked worriedly from one face to the other. He was thoroughly scared, and he was wishing he'd never gotten into this. But there was no help for it now.

Besides, instead of being scared, he

should be thinking of Patch lying dead out there in the street. He should be thinking that his father could then rest easy in his grave.

Locke reached under the bar and brought out a short, double-barreled shotgun. It was a ten gauge and was fairly new, using center fire and red paper shells. Locke broke the gun, loaded it and snapped it shut. He handed the gun and a handful of cartridges to Will.

Will took them. He was more at home with a shot gun than with the little nickel-plated pistol in his pocket. He'd hunted rabbits and quail with his father out on the prairie beyond the town.

Phil Miller went into the back room of the saloon, where the card games were played evenings, and returned a few moments later carrying two rifles. Locke got a holstered gun and cartridge belt from beneath the bar and belted the gun around his waist after taking off his white apron. He said, "We'd better go out the back door. We don't want anyone warning Patch."

He went to the front door and closed and locked the two solid doors against the swinging doors. Then he led the way through the back room and out into the alley. He snapped a padlock on the back door, then led the three men up the alley toward the warehouse across from the jail.

Reaching the place, Locke nodded toward the rickety rear stairway. Phil and Chris climbed the stairs ahead of Will. Will stopped at the second-floor landing, but the other two continued on up to the roof. Will could hear their footsteps resounding hollowly above his head as he went into the long, dusty hallway, startled to see footprints in the dust ahead of him.

And suddenly the truth came to him. Those footprints had been made by his father, earlier today. His father had come up here before he had chosen the passageway as a hiding place.

Seeing his father's footprints gave Will an eerie feeling. He ducked quickly into an office that fronted on the street. He crossed to the window and scrubbed at a spot on the glass with his hand. He could clearly see the marshal's office and the jail across the street. It seemed very close from here.

He unfastened the window catch and tugged at the window, trying to open it. It was stuck and wouldn't budge. He went to the next window and unfastened it similarly. This time the window opened slightly, far enough to slide the shotgun muzzle through, far enough to look over the barrel at the doorway of the jail.

With his knees shaking, Will knelt on the floor. He was still too high, so he sat down cross-legged. This was just right, he discovered. He slid the shotgun muzzle through the window, opening and sighting the gun on the jail.

This was as good as he could do. He was as ready as he would ever be. He didn't see how he could miss the marshal when he came out the door.

Chapter 16

Dan began to fill the woodbox in the kitchen. He made half a dozen trips before it was completely full. After that he hitched up the brown mare to the Jorgensens' wagon and drove down to the loading pens beyond the depot. Ma Jorgensen had made a deal with the town to buy the wood in the old corrals, and whenever their supply at the boardinghouse ran low, Dan would haul a load of poles and posts from the depot to the boardinghouse.

It was well past noon. The sun was starting down the western sky. Dan cocked his head at it and wished the day was over.

He tied the mare and began to pull the fence apart, loading the poles on the wagon as he pulled them loose. He had not worked long before he began to sweat heavily.

He stopped to rest a moment and stared down at his boots. There was a lot of confusion in him today. The lines of right and wrong didn't seem clear-cut any more. Until today he'd thought Patch could do no wrong, but it was hard to understand how shooting Mr. Oxley could be right. Or how humiliating Mr. Trinidad and booting him out of the marshal's office could be right either, for that matter.

Dan raised a hand reflectively and rubbed the side of his face where Patch's open hand had struck him. That had been a pretty darned hard slap. He supposed he'd deserved it for sassing Patch, but that didn't make it any easier to take. Dan was glad no one had seen him slapped. At least no one but him and Patch knew about the slap.

Dan went back to loading poles, a thin frown staying on his face. Why did things have to go and get spoiled this way? Like the scuffed places on the boots, the shine seemed to be gone from everything today.

He finished loading the wagon and climbed up on the seat. He drove back to the boardinghouse and pulled the wagon in beside the shed. He got down and began to unload the poles.

He had purposely avoided driving along Elm on the way to the depot or returning from it, but now he wished he'd driven past the jail. He wondered if the townsmen had given up yet trying to fire Patch. If they hadn't, he wondered what they'd do next.

The wagon was about half unloaded when he became conscious of someone watching him. Glancing up, he saw Hilda standing at the corner of the shed. He stopped and wiped the sweat off his forehead with a sleeve. Hilda said, "Guess what."

He stared at her irritably. There was a strange, almost triumphant smile on her mouth. He said, "I don't know. What?"

"Mr. Patch and Mrs. Quintana just got married. Over in the parsonage on Oak."

He stared at her unbelievingly. He growled, "Who do you think you're foolin,? Patch wouldn't marry her. Besides, why would he want to marry anyone?"

"I don't know, but it's true. Mrs. Stanton is sitting in the parlor with Ma right now. She was one of the witnesses, she said."

Dan glared. "You're lyin'. You're just tryin' to make me mad. Patch wouldn't marry her!"

Hilda said, "You don't have to get so mad. I didn't bring the story anyhow. Mrs. Stanton did. If you want to use words like that, you can just go use them on her."

"Maybe I will. Maybe I just will." He hated Hilda suddenly, hated her for the lie she'd just repeated so triumphantly to him. Patch wouldn't do a thing like that, especially today. He glared at her angrily. "Go on, get out of here. I don't even want to talk to you."

The triumphant look was gone from her face, and her eyes were stricken now.

Suddenly they filled with tears. Dan yelled, "Go on! Go on!"

Still Hilda did not move. Dan shouted, "I'll prove it to you, by God! I'll go down and ask Mr. Patch myself!"

He tied the mare to the shed. He whirled and ran toward the jail. He didn't know whether Hilda was following him or not, and he didn't care. He felt sick at his stomach. He felt awful, like somebody had slugged him in his guts.

He'd heard talk about Claire Quintana in the boardinghouse, mostly sly talk about what a woman she'd be if only a man could get next to her. Trouble was, they said, she was Frank Patch's girl, and nobody would dare try cutting in on him even if Claire would be agreeable.

Dan hadn't paid much attention to the talk. You heard all kinds of talk at the boardinghouse. There wasn't a single woman in town that didn't get talked about by that bunch. Even some of the married ones had some pretty raunchy things said about them.

Besides, he'd never seen Patch with Claire. He'd never even seen Patch speak to her.

Dan was out of breath by the time he reached Elm. Glancing behind, he saw that Hilda was following. She raised a hand and called to him when she saw him turn his head, but he didn't stop.

Now he was scared. He was scared to go on and scared to stop. What if it were true? What if Patch had married Claire?

There were a few people on the street, but mostly the town seemed to drowse in the afternoon sun. Patch's big black horse stood tied at the rail in front of the jail. Dan stopped running when he reached the gate. Out of breath, sweating and dusty from the work he had been doing, he started up the path to the door.

He felt like a fool now because he didn't know what he was going to say. What the marshal did was none of his business anyway. He had no right to criticize.

He stopped and glanced behind him

again. Hilda was less than half a block away. She was running, holding up the hem of her skirt in front so that she wouldn't trip on it. She screamed something to him, but he didn't understand what it was.

For an instant he considered ducking through the weeds beside the jail and escaping at the rear. He was afraid to confront Patch and ask him if the story about him and Mrs. Quintana was true. But he couldn't let Hilda know he was afraid.

He opened the jail door and ducked inside. He slammed it behind him and put his back to it, as though to hold it shut and keep Hilda out. Patch glanced up from his desk questioningly.

There were a lot of things in Patch's face, changing, conflicting expressions that Dan didn't wholly understand. But Patch was silent, waiting for him to speak.

Hilda was sorry she'd told Dan about

228

Patch's marriage to Claire Quintana almost as soon as the words were out of her mouth. Hilda didn't completely understand her own petulance in telling him in the first place. She supposed that, actually, she was a little jealous of Dan's regard for Patch. She had wanted to show Dan that Patch was a lot less than Dan had thought. She had wanted to make him turn away from Patch.

But the effect of her words on Dan made her instantly regret having said anything. His face lost color; his eyes became pinched; his mouth firmed; and his words came out recklessly. She'd never seen him so upset before.

And when he tied the mare and ran toward the marshal's office to ask Patch if the story was really true . . . Hilda would have done anything to be able to recall her words. Dan would have found out about Patch's marriage sooner or later anyway. But he'd have found out from someone else. He wouldn't have blamed Hilda, as though she was personally responsible for it.

But the damage was done and could not now be undone. All she could do now was follow Dan and be close when he found out that the story was really true. She could be there for him to talk to when he finally wanted to talk.

She ran after him, hampered by her long skirts, even though she held the front hem up. Dan gained steadily, however, and by the time he had reached Elm she was half a block behind.

She saw him stop just inside the gate leading to the jail and look back at her. She cried out to him to stop, but he either didn't hear or just plain ignored her plea. He disappeared into the jail.

There was no use in Hilda's running now. There was no use exhausting what remained of her breath. Dan would be in the jail a little while, and it was a place Hilda couldn't go. Her mother would have a fit if she heard that Hilda had gone inside the jail. It was almost as bad as going into one of the saloons. Hilda wasn't even supposed to be below Texas Street.

She slowed to a walk and approached the jail that way. She glanced around her guiltily, hoping no one who might later tell her mother she had been here would see her now. Her eye caught movement on the roof of the red-brick building across from the jail.

She turned her head and stared. There was a man up on that roof, and he had a rifle in his hands.

Suddenly another movement caught her eye. There was another gun poking out of one of the second-story windows across the street from the jail. The window had been raised barely enough to accommodate it.

She glanced away, fear turning her cold. There could be only one reason for men with guns across the street. They were going to try to kill the marshal just as Mr. Oxley had tried to do earlier. There were at least two men, and maybe more.

Suddenly all she could think of was Dan. Dan was there inside the jail. Dan might be mistaken for the marshal when he opened the door to come out again. Dan could be shot and killed, and his death would be her fault. It was her fault that he was here, her fault because if she'd kept her mouth shut about Patch and Claire Quintana, Dan would still be at the boardinghouse unloading poles.

She began to run again. She screamed, "Dan! Dan! Don't come out here, Dan! There are men with guns across the street!"

She reached the gate that opened onto the path leading to the jail. She turned in and ran blindly toward the door. She tripped on her skirt and sprawled forward, sobbing, terrified.

She heard the door to the jail being flung open. And suddenly there was a roaring in her ears – of voices – of guns. There was a roaring, and she was falling, falling into a pit, falling into unconsciousness.

Patch stared at Dan, who stood with his back against the door. He could see the sweat on young Dan's face, combining

232

with the dust. He could see the way it had stained Dan's shirt. He could hear the way Dan's breath panted the way a dog's does when it has been running hard. He waited patiently for Dan to speak, wondering what could have put that look of wildness into the boy's eyes.

Patch had faintly heard Hilda's shrill voice half a block up the street and had wondered whose it was. But then the voice was silent so he continued to study Dan and wait for the boy to speak.

Dan cleared his throat. He choked, "You . . . you . . ." still too short of breath to speak coherently.

Patch said, "Wait a minute, boy. Wait 'til you've got your breath."

Dan nodded. His chest rose and fell. Suddenly there was a scream outside. It was a terrified scream, a scream of fear. Patch was on his feet instantly.

He charged across the office, reaching the door before Dan had time to turn around. Patch's gun was in his hand, his thumb on the hammer, his forefinger through the trigger guard. He brushed

Dan aside with one sweep of his powerful arm, sending the boy staggering across the room to crash against the stove. Patch yanked the door open and plunged outside.

He saw Hilda crumpled in the path. He plunged toward her, starting the gun back toward its holster as he did.

The first shot from across the street, a rifle shot from the roof, grazed his shoulder and thudded into the stone wall of the jail, shattering and showering the doorway with bits of lead and stone. Patch veered as though he had been stung by a bee, his gun now coming up, his eyes rising to the roof of the building across the street.

Another rifle roared, and this bullet tore into the thigh muscles of Patch's right leg. It dumped him neatly fifteen feet from where Hilda lay at the exact instant that the ten gauge roared from the open window directly across the street.

The second barrel roared, like an echo of the first. A rain of buckshot kicked up

234

dust spurts from the gate to the door of the jail, pelted the stone wall of the jail, and rattled along the picket fence and the boardwalk in front of it.

Patch took a pellet deep into his back muscles on the left side. He took another in his rump. Stung, aware that he might die in seconds, he raised himself and put a bullet into the window across the street right above the smoking shotgun muzzle there.

The tinkle of shattering glass briefly filled the air. The shotgun muzzle disappeared. Patch glanced at the rooftop again.

Seeing movement there, he snapped a shot at it. His bullet struck a brick cornice and ricocheted into space, buzzing like a bee. The shot showered the rifleman with stinging particles of brick.

Patch was like a wounded grizzly now. It would take a heavy bullet in a vital spot to put him down. Limping, punching out empties and reloading by feel as he ran, he vaulted Hilda lying sprawled in the path and went into the street. He kept his eyes on the roof of the building across the street, but the riflemen had disappeared. Nothing moved in the shattered second-story window where the man with the shotgun had been.

Patch ran for the passageway from which Oxley had shot him earlier. Blood was a gushing warmth on his thigh and a sticky wetness on his back and on the seat of his pants. Damn them anyway, he thought. They didn't have to shoot a man where he sat down.

He reached the passageway and plunged into it. He was forced to turn sideways to negotiate it. He reached the other end and whirled toward the rickety stairway leading to the offices on the second floor and beyond them to the roof.

He could hear a crashing sound in the alley as someone blundered through a pile of scattered trash, but he didn't turn toward the sound. For some reason, pride perhaps, he wanted the one who had blasted him with that damned shotgun. His rump stung like fire, and so did his back. He wanted the man with that scattergun.

The door at the head of the stairs flung open suddenly. Patch's eye caught a flash of movement there, the shape of a man with a shotgun in his hands.

The man stood there for a fraction of a second before seeing Patch and trying to duck to one side. Patch's gun, raised and ready, fired as though the trigger had been pulled automatically. The bullet sped unerringly to its mark.

The man was driven back, out of sight in the dark hallway. His shotgun clattered on the landing, then skidded off to hit and break on the ground below.

Patch was running now, running toward those stairs, taking them by twos when he reached them. He gained the top and plunged into the dusty, abandoned hallway.

He recognized Will Oxley instantly, although he had not recognized the boy moments before in the doorway. He knew that Will was dead.

There was a big, spreading spot of blood on the front of Will Oxley's shirt. The town's determination to be rid of Patch had cost another life. Damn them, damn them, why didn't they give up?

Chapter 17

Gunfire roared in the street. It lasted only seconds, the seconds it took for Dan Joslyn to fight his way to his feet again and stumble dazedly to the door.

Staring into the street, he saw Patch running diagonally across it toward the passageway where Oxley had hidden himself earlier. He saw Hilda crumpled on the walk.

There was an acrid smell in the air, the smell of powdersmoke. A thin cloud of it was drifting down toward the depot, both from the street and from the second-story window of the building across from the jail. The window now was shattered and lay in pieces, glittering in the sun.

Dan stared at Hilda unbelievingly. She had either fainted, or she was hurt. He was scared; he was terrified. He wanted to turn and run more than anything else in the world. But he forced himself to walk toward her. He forced himself to kneel at her side.

Her face was like ivory, or like wax, and it had a smudge of dust on the right cheek and temple. There was dust in her yellow hair. On the front of her dress there was a scarlet stain of blood.

Dan felt as though a mule had kicked him in the stomach. He felt light-headed, as though he was going to faint. He started to lay a hand on her chest, then withdrew as though he had been burned. He picked up her wrist instead.

He groped around for her pulse. His hands were shaking so violently he could scarcely hold her wrist. His teeth began to chatter helplessly. His body felt as cold as ice.

He couldn't find a pulse. He looked up and around frantically, his eyes terri-fied. He needed help but didn't know what to do. He couldn't find Hilda's pulse, but she couldn't be dead. She just couldn't be dead. She had been alive, and running, and crying out to him less than a minute ago.

People were now coming cautiously into the street. First, they poked their heads out of their doors, then stepped outside nervously, then advanced slowly when they saw no one in the street.

Claire and Jake had come out of the Goliad seconds earlier. Claire was running now, running toward the jail. Jake was shambling along behind her, losing ground though trying to keep up with Claire.

Claire turned in at the gate, rushed to Hilda and dropped to the ground at her side. She took one look at Dan, then snatched Hilda's wrist from his shaking hands. She held it for a moment, then carefully laid it down again. Gently she looked at Dan. "She's dead, Dan. I'm sorry. I'm so terribly sorry."

Dan struggled to his feet. It didn't seem possible to him that Hilda was dead. It seemed like a nightmare from which he would awaken to find Hilda alive and all right once more. He stared at Claire, wondering if it was true that she was Patch's wife. That didn't seem to matter now. Nothing seemed to matter any more. He wanted to cry. He wanted to bury his face in Claire and cry as he had when he was a little boy.

A crowd was forming now. Sayre was there, and Lou Trinidad, and a dozen others including Jake, Claire's bartender at the Goliad. Patch came running across the street. He stopped just inside the gate, stared down at Hilda's body, then up at Claire and Dan. He said, "God! I thought she had only fainted. I didn't know . . ."

Dan felt recklessness rising in him. He felt as if he had to blame somebody for Hilda's death. If he didn't, he might have to face the fact that, except for him, except for his childish quarrel with her, she would still be safe at home. He said, "It's your fault, damn you! It's all your fault! If you weren't so damn set on keeping your lousy marshal's job, this wouldn't have happened and Hilda would still be alive!"

242

Claire said sharply, "Dan! You've got no right to say that to him! And besides, it isn't true. Frank can't help it if someone tries to shoot him down."

Dan's voice rose. He looked at Claire defiantly, then at Patch again. "If you'd of quit, it wouldn't have happened! Would it? Would it?"

"Maybe not, Dan, but that doesn't make it my fault. What was Hilda doing down here anyway?"

Dan wouldn't answer that. He couldn't answer, not without admitting he was partly to blame for Hilda's death. He screeched irrationally, "You did it! You did it! It's your fault! You're a damn lousy killer and a murderer!"

Patch's hand swung. For a second time today it struck the side of Dan's face, rocking his head violently to one side, setting his ears to ringing. Dan shut his mouth and stared silently at Patch. His shock, his terror, his grief . . . all these things turned suddenly to hate, hate that blazed now from his eyes.

It shocked Patch into immobility, into

silence. He stared back at Dan, his eyes narrowed as though from pain. Suddenly Dan whirled and ran. He ran through the weeds alongside the jail and into the alley in back. He disappeared from sight.

Patch looked at Claire. Tears had spilled over from Claire's eyes and were now running across her cheeks. But there was understanding in her brimming eyes, understanding and pity and something else that Patch had never seen in a woman's eyes before. He mumbled something about getting a shotgun and hurried inside the jail. In a moment he was back, carrying a sawed-off double-barrel, stuffing a handful of shells into the pocket of his pants. Claire said, "Frank!"

He turned his head and looked at her. There was anger in him now, a vengeful anger that she knew would not be denied. She said only, "Be careful, Frank."

He nodded shortly and ran out through the gate. The townsmen gave way before him, their faces white, their eyes showing fear not only of what was happening but also of Patch himself.

There had been two men on the roof across the street. Will Oxley had been in the upstairs window. Someone else had been waiting in the passageway but had lost his nerve and had run away after the shooting had begun. Patch wanted three men, but he didn't know which three. Will Oxley could have told him, but Will had been dead when he reached the boy.

Patch stopped suddenly in the middle of the street. A hasty glance downstreet revealed something unusual to him. The doors of the Alamo were closed and locked from the inside.

That simple fact told him who two of the men were that had ambushed him. One was Locke. Another was Locke's alternate bartender, Phil Miller, who would have been keeping the Alamo open for Locke if he had not been in this, too. The third ... Patch couldn't guess who the third might be, but when he found Locke and Miller, he might find the third man, too.

Those three were going to die. Those three were going to die for Hilda's death, and for Will Oxley's death as well. Will hadn't had the guts to do something like this on his own. He'd never have tried taking a shot at the marshal if he hadn't been egged on by someone else.

Locke, Miller and the third man were going to die by his gun, Patch told himself, because otherwise they'd go free. The autopsy would reveal that Hilda died of buckshot pellets fired from Will Oxley's gun. Will Oxley was dead, so he couldn't answer for her death. Legally that would leave the other three men in the clear, particularly since no one knew for sure who they were nor could anyone prove they had been involved in the ambush. All they had to do was get back to the Alamo and get inside. They'd be in the clear.

Patch whirled toward the Alamo. They weren't going to reach that sanctuary if he could stop them. They weren't going to get inside and get rid of their guns. They were going to answer for their crime.

The town of Cottonwood Springs had one undertaker and a single hearse. Twenty minutes after Hilda had been shot, before anyone had notified her mother that she was dead, the hearse pulled up in front of the jail, and Arch Brandt got down. He opened the rear doors and slid the stretcher out. One of the men standing outside the fence helped him and the two carried the stretcher into the tiny, grassy front yard of the jail. They laid the canvas down beside Hilda. Arch stooped and lifted her upper body. The other man lifted her feet. They laid her on the stretcher, and Brandt covered her with a sheet. They raised the stretcher, carried it to the hearse and slid it inside. Claire could still see Hilda through the oval windows on the side of the hearse, but Hilda was just a body now, covered with a sheet. She was not Hilda Jorgensen any longer.

Brandt got into the seat, motioning

for the other man to join him, and the two drove away in the direction of Ma Jorgensen's boardinghouse.

The crowd began to disperse. Claire looked down the street and saw Patch stop in front of the Alamo. She saw him raise a booted foot and kick the doors violently. On the third kick they sprang open, and Patch plunged inside. Claire held her breath a moment, waiting for the sound of gunfire, but it didn't come. There was only the muted talk of the people standing around in front of the jail. There was only the muffled sobbing of a woman in the crowd.

One by one the people slowly walked away. Once in a while one would look worriedly toward the Alamo, but nothing seemed to be happening there. Patch had not reappeared. Apparently neither Locke nor Phil Miller had returned to the Alamo, or something would be happening. It was obvious Patch thought Locke and Miller were the ones who had been in on the ambush attempt with Will Oxley, and Claire agreed with her husband. Proving the conspiracy, however, would be something else, she knew, unless the conspirators could be made to give themselves away.

She closed the door of the jail. Jake was waiting for her by the gate, a worried look on his face. "You want me to get a gun and go help him, ma'am? I might not be much good, but I sure don't mind givin' it a try."

She smiled gratefully at him. "Not yet, Jake. Maybe later, if he asks for help. So far I think he's all right. Maybe the town will give up now, particularly if he gets the others that were in on it with Will."

Jake nodded, obviously relieved. Claire walked back toward the Goliad, keeping her eyes on the open doors of the Alamo as she walked. She wondered where the riflemen had gone after they had escaped from the roof of the warehouse across the street from the jail. Probably they'd just run, trying to put as much distance between themselves and Patch as possible. Probably they'd run to the bed of Cottonwood Creek and were hiding there. Sooner or later though, they'd realize that hiding out would just draw attention to them and pin complicity in the crime on them. When they realized that, they'd return to the Alamo.

They'd find Patch waiting for them there, and that was sure to be a shock. They'd probably give themselves away – either by shooting it out with Patch or by trying to run away again. And that was exactly what Patch was counting on them to do. Unless they involved themselves, he didn't have a chance of obtaining a conviction in court. Nobody but Hilda had seen them, and neither she nor Will Oxley could talk.

Claire and Jake reached the Goliad and went inside. Jake went behind the bar and poured himself a drink.

Claire stayed at the window, staring at the open doors of the Alamo. She realized she was listening intently – for the sound of gunfire coming from the place.

She told herself that she had confidence in Patch. He would get safely through the day. She had confidence in his ability to take care of himself. But a little, nagging worry stayed in the back of her mind anyway. It could have been Patch instead of Hilda who had died a little while ago. It could so easily have been Patch.

And even if he did get through the day . . . no matter what he thought right now, he was going to have to quit because this town wasn't going to give up. The townsmen were going to make Patch quit, or they were going to carry him out of his office on a slab.

Chapter 18

Inside the Alamo, Patch was like a caged mountain lion. Back and forth he paced, back and forth, as silently as his boots allowed. He had checked the back door and knew that it was locked. Now he crossed to the front doors and closed them the way they had been before he had broken the lock, securing them. He wanted everything to look exactly as Locke and Phil Miller had left it earlier. He wanted nothing to make them suspect anything was wrong.

Patch was fully aware that proving complicity against them would be almost impossible. Only Hilda had seen them on the roof. Will Oxley, who might have involved them had he lived long enough to talk, was dead. Patch knew the only chance of making Locke and Miller pay for their crime was by making them put up a fight when he surprised them on their return.

Besides, he was virtually certain Hilda had been killed by the buckshot from Will Oxley's gun. So, proving direct complicity would be difficult even if Patch could prove the two men had been on the roof, even if he could prove they had been in league with Will.

Sooner or later Locke and Miller were going to realize that their absence from the Alamo and from the crowd on the street was pointing the finger of guilt at them. When they did, they wouldn't be able to get back to the saloon fast enough.

When the hearse arrived, Patch stopped pacing long enough to watch Hilda carried out and put into it. The hearse drove away in the direction of Ma Jorgensen's boardinghouse.

His eyes narrowed with pain that seemed almost physical as he thought of the shock to Ma Jorgensen, having her daughter brought home this way. He should have gone to the boardinghouse ahead of the hearse and should have told Ma what had happened to Hilda. But if he had, those responsible for Hilda's death would have escaped paying the penalty for it. He was sure Ma would understand that, when she recovered from her grief.

The hearse disappeared around the corner, and Patch resumed his pacing nervously. He was both shocked and appalled at what had happened in Cottonwood Springs today. It seemed impossible that three good people lay dead, two killed by his own hand in defense of his life, the third killed accidentally because she happened to be in the way.

Patch scowled savagely at the floor. Was he so bad that such measures were justified? He shook his head.

Briefly he considered quitting the job, and asked himself soberly if he should quit. Would his leaving restore peace to the shocked and grieving town? No, it was too late now to quit. If he had been going to quit, he should have done so early this morning, when Sayre and his delegation first brought their demand to him.

Three killers were loose in the town right now, three men as guilty of Hilda's death as though they had actually pulled the trigger themselves. If Patch quit, as the mayor insisted, those three would go scot free. Hilda's death would remain unavenged.

No. He couldn't quit. Not now. Perhaps the time would never come when he could quit. Perhaps the only way the townsmen would ever get him out of the marshal's office would be to carry him out on that stretcher in the hearse, covered with a sheet.

Patch heard a sound at the back door and realized instantly that someone was fooling with the lock. He stepped into the back room and waited silently, hearing muffled voices, the scuffing sound of boots, and at last the squeaking of hinges as the alley door opened.

Locke was talking. ". . . get on in here and open the damned place up. Phil, you and Chris get out on the street and mix with the crowd. After a little while ask somebody down here for a drink."

Phil Miller stepped into the semi-darkness of the saloon's back room, and Chris Hogg followed him. Patch thought triumphantly that now he knew who the third man was. He had all three of them.

Phil and Chris stopped dead when they saw Patch standing there. Locke bumped into them from the rear, muttered a curse, then saw why they had stopped.

Patch drew his gun from its holster and fired. But he had fired too quickly for accuracy. The bullet tore into the floor at Chris Hogg's feet.

Patch tried to shoot at Locke, but Chris and Phil were in the way. He roared, "Hold it, damn the three of you! You're under arrest for the murder of Hilda Jorgensen!"

Phil Miller's answer was to raise and fire his rifle directly at Patch's face. Although the bullet missed the marshal's head by an inch, buzzing past his ear like an angry bee, the concussion of the muzzle blast was deafening. And the cloud of powdersmoke billowed squarely into his face.

His skin felt as though scalding water had been dumped on it. For an instant he was blind, clawing at his face and eyes with his free hand, cursing savagely beneath his breath, trying to see well enough to shoot.

Instinctively, he ducked aside, protecting himself, trying to hide until he could defend himself. He heard the excited voices of the three men and their scuffling, retreating feet. After that he heard gravel grating as they ran down the alley behind the Alamo.

In spite of the pain he was in, in spite of his powder-burned face, Patch felt a wild elation sweep over him. He had his proof. He knew for certain now who the three he wanted were. They had fired at him and had admitted guilt and complicity when they did.

All he had to do now was track them

down, a job he was well fitted for. All he had to do was to hunt them down like the animals they were.

They'd never surrender to him. He knew they'd fight until the last one of them was dead. And that was exactly what he wanted.

He could see a little more clearly now, though his eyes still burned like fire and he had to keep blinking rapidly. With his face black from burnt powder, with his eyes streaming tears, he charged into the alley behind the Alamo.

Instantly a rifle roared at the end of the alley. The bullet tore a furrow in the dirt at Patch's feet, then ricocheted noisily away.

He ducked into a vacant lot next to the saloon. His gun was in his hand, hammer back and held there with his thumb. His vision was improving all the time as tears washed the powder from his eyes. But the burns they had sustained kept the pain constant and kept the tears flowing enough to blur everything.

He couldn't fight anyone right now, he

thought. He couldn't see well enough to fight one man, let alone three such as these. But he could keep close enough to them so that when his vision cleared . . .

Patch plunged into the alley. He charged down it, running hard but light in spite of the boots he wore.

He reached the end of the alley, stopping just short of the boardwalk and peered out cautiously.

Instantly from the direction of Elm a rifle roared. The bullet struck the wall beyond Patch, embedding itself in the brick.

He ducked back, rounded the building and came out through a long passage-way between two buildings onto Elm Street.

He knew he must be cautious but the realization didn't change the way he burst out of the passageway into Elm. He thought of Hilda Jorgensen, dead because these three men and Will Oxley had ambushed him.

From the door of the livery stable a rifle opened on him, the bullets striking the street in front of him and ricocheting up the street. Patch heard glass tinkle behind him as he ran and hoped the townspeople had sense enough to curb their curiosity enough to stay indoors. He didn't want anyone else killed accidentally.

The man in the livery barn was there to hold him back until the other two could escape. He saw them running ahead of him. They reached the depot and disappeared behind it in the direction of the cattle pens.

Patch was willing to bet the man in the livery barn was Chris Hogg. Locke and Miller would stick together, using the cowboy to make possible their escape.

Patch ran straight toward the livery barn, zigzagging as he ran. He ran toward the door and the half-seen rifleman, and when the marshal was but a hundred yards away, he raised his gun to shoot.

The rifleman's nerve broke, as Patch had known it would. The man turned and ran toward the rear of the livery barn. Patch burst into the front of the barn as the man tried to run out the rear.

Patch stopped and fired immediately, steadying himself enough to be accurate.

The running man seemed to stumble. Then, as though driven by some powerful force from behind, he dived out the rear door of the livery barn, skidding as he hit the ground outside. Patch ran the length of the barn, burst through the gaping rear door and stopped at the prone man's side. He turned the man over with his boot.

It was Chris Hogg, as he had thought, and Chris was dead. There was a trickle of blood coming from one corner of his mouth. His chest was still.

Patch punched the empties from his gun and reloaded automatically as he went back into the livery barn. Horses were plunging and stamping nervously in their stalls. One nickered shrilly at him and tried to rear in spite of the halter rope. Patch said soothingly, "Whoa, now. Take it easy there. Nothin' to get all riled up about. It's over as far as you're concerned."

He knew he'd make a better target on a horse. He also knew he'd be faster and have more mobility. Besides, he was aware of the psychological advantage a man on horseback has over his adversaries. He stopped at one of the stalls, untied the halter rope of a strong-looking brown gelding and led the animal to the front of the livery barn. He snatched a bridle from a peg and put it on the horse. He vaulted to the horse's bare back and thundered out through the open doors into the street.

He wheeled the horse immediately toward the cattle pens. He couldn't see his quarry yet, but he knew exactly where it was. He knew the two would shoot at him as soon as he came into range.

He dug heels into the horse's flanks, and the animal seemed to spring forward. Horse and rider sailed over the railroad tracks, wheeled around the nearest loading chute and pounded into an alleyway between the pens at a dead run.

A rifle roared almost in Patch's face, but he was past the rifleman before he could think of stopping or even of slowing down. Patch yanked the horse aside into another alleyway opening off this one at right angles and flung himself from the horse.

Gun in hand, the marshal ran back to the main alleyway and poked his head out cautiously. A rifle roared instantly, but it was farther away than he had expected and had a different sound than the first one. The bullet tore a shower of splinters from a nearby pole. When its sound had died away, he heard the sound of running feet. He poked his head out again, this time snapping a quick shot in the direction of the rifleman.

Patch understood immediately what Locke and Miller's plan of action was. One would fire at him while the other retreated. Then the one who had retreated would open up on the marshal

263

while the first man retreated. This way, the two men meant to work their way back into town.

Patch frowned lightly, wondering why they had run from town in the first place if they had intended only to return again. The answer was obvious immediately. They had panicked when he surprised them in the back room of the Alamo. Now they'd had time to think. Locke's mind had gone to work. Locke knew if he could return the fight to town, he would probably get support from other disgruntled members of the community. Others who wanted to be rid of Patch would help him and Miller.

The hell of it was, Patch thought wryly, Locke probably was right. But Patch had no intention of letting Locke and Miller work their way back into town, if he could stop them. He wanted this fight to end right here in the cattle pens, where no more innocent people could get hurt.

He returned to the horse and mounted. He kicked the willing, excited animal into a run, wheeled into the main alleyway and headed straight for the depot.

Chapter 19

Instantly a rifle opened up on him from the window of the depot. He could see the other man run past the depot and enter Elm. Patch leaned low on the horse's back so as to present as small a target as possible. He snapped a shot at the depot window, but all he did was shatter the glass over the hidden marksman's head. The rifle roared again.

His horse stumbled and fell. He somersaulted, throwing Patch forward. Patch rolled for thirty feet before he came to rest. The rifle in the depot window roared again. This bullet showered Patch with dirt and forced him to jump frantically to his feet and sprint for the corner of the building.

The first man, who had run uptown, was now out of sight. But almost immediately he began firing from behind a building nearly a block above the depot. His aim wasn't expert, and it was good enough to keep Patch pinned down.

The man in the depot came out now and sprinted uptown toward the spot where his companion was hiding. Angered, Patch stuck his head out and fired unthinkingly at the running man.

His bullet struck the dirt in the street a foot to one side of the man and ricocheted, smashing a window somewhere uptown. Patch couldn't see the window that the bullet smashed, but he could hear the tinkle of broken glass. With an angry curse, he ducked and reloaded automatically, without thinking.

Locke and Miller had succeeded in what they had set out to do. They had reached the town – a shelter from which they could shoot at Patch but at which he in turn dared not shoot. He felt a responsibility toward the townspeople who were not involved in this battle, even if Locke and Phil Miller did not.

Scowling, Patch tried to decide what he must do. He had to outsmart Locke and Miller; he had to outthink them; he had to beat them at their own game.

Above all, he did not dare let them get away with Hilda's murder. He did not dare let them flaunt their lawlessness and impugn his authority to enforce the law.

Gun still in hand, Patch ran along the platform to the rear of the depot. From here, he sprinted to the bed of Cottonwood Creek. Trotting tirelessly, he followed the brushy bed of the creek until he reached the upper part of town.

Now he climbed out of the ravine, working back to Elm Street a block above Texas Street.

He had regained the advantage over the two, he realized. He had regained the initiative. He knew approximately where they were, but now they had not the slightest idea where he was.

Ducking from building to building, sometimes using the street, sometimes the alleys, he worked his way back to the center of town. At Elm and Texas streets he stopped.

Elm Street was deserted. Now, he thought bitterly, the townspeople could have helped him. They could have let him know where the two killers were. Even if the townspeople didn't feel qualified to intervene actively, they could do that much.

But no one showed himself. No one offered Patch any help. although the marshal knew that a number of the townsmen could see him from where they were.

At least, now, he would not have to fire in the direction of the heavily populated part of town. At least his gun could kill no one accidentally.

With his back to a building wall, Patch squatted comfortably on his heels. He holstered his gun, dug out his pipe and tobacco and filled the pipe deliberately. He lighted it and puffed heartily. Time would work for him although the men of the town would not. With every passing minute, Locke and Miller were going to get more nervous and on edge. By the time fifteen minutes had passed, they'd be so damned nervous they'd shoot at anything.

Squatting against the wall, smoking his pipe, Patch began to feel his wounds stiffening. His pants were stuck to his leg by drying blood. His shirt was stuck to his back. The grazed place on his shoulder burned, and the thigh wound ached ferociously.

The shallow wounds didn't really amount to much. The shotgun pellets could be removed fairly easily. Nor did the bullet burn on his shoulder amount to anything. But the thigh wound was different. The rifle bullet had damaged muscles, and if he ever stopped moving for very long . . . that wound would keep him from walking if it ever got a chance to stiffen.

He got up immediately and began pacing back and forth, limping at first, gradually loosening up enough so that his limp was not noticeable. He felt the thigh wound begin to bleed again.

He took his pipe out of his mouth and

knocked out the ashes against the heel of his hand. The two men he was hunting ought to come prowling past here soon. It had been almost twenty minutes, he judged, since he had reached this spot and stopped to wait.

He caught sight of movement in a doorway across the street, as someone peered out and then hastily ducked back. The movement told him what he needed to know. One of the two, was coming up the street looking for him.

Patch drew his gun, checked the loads and thumbed the hammer back. He waited, with seeming indolence, but as ready as a cat waiting for a mouse to come out of its hole. And then, making use of the element of surprise, Patch stepped from the building corner into sight.

There were two of them. Locke was on the far side of the street, carrying a shotgun now, a double-barrel, perhaps the same one Will Oxley had killed Hilda with. Miller was nearer, carrying a rifle, walking a little crouched as though

271

expecting Patch to materialize out of nothing in front of him.

Patch fired at Locke instantly and saw his bullet whirl Locke around. The shotgun roared, first one barrel, then the other. The first charge blew out a second-story window behind Locke. The second knocked out the doorglass where Patch had seen someone appear and disappear only moments before.

Patch turned his attention to Miller, knowing Locke was no longer a threat, at least not until Locke could reload his gun. Miller had swung slightly toward Patch. Miller held his gun at his hip and fired from there. The bullet missed the marshal, hit a brick wall and ricocheted, then crashed through the plate-glass window of the hotel lobby.

Patch fired, too, but not before he had raised his gun and taken careful aim. There were enough wild bullets flying around without his adding to them.

Miller doubled over as though a fist had slammed into his stomach. His rifle clattered to the dust at his feet. He hugged his belly for what seemed a long, long time. Then he fell forward, jerking a couple of times, and lay still.

Patch swung toward Locke again. Without taking time to try to reload the shotgun, Locke suddenly turned and ran, zigzagging as he went. He crossed a vacant lot and disappeared into a trash-littered alley with Patch in hot pursuit.

Chester Sayre came to the door of his dry goods store and stared out at the street. It was littered with broken glass along both sides. He could see Phil Miller lying almost in the center of the street, where Miller had fallen only minutes before.

Other shopkeepers were beginning to peer cautiously into the street. Sayre beckoned to several of them, and they came out of their stores, running to join him inside the dry goods store.

The faces of all were soberly serious. Several of them were pale. The hands of one were shaking violently. Sayre said, "This has got to be stopped. It's got to be stopped now, before anyone else gets killed. That damned Patch only seems to know one way of doing things, and that's with his goddam gun."

Ivan Stanek said, "Who's goin' to stop him? You?"

Sayre glanced at him irritably. "We won't get any place getting nasty with each other. Maybe Lou Trinidad could stop him if there was anyone here with guts enough to go up to the courthouse for Lou Trinidad."

Stanek flushed. "All right, all right. I'll go after him." He went to the front of the store, peered into the street, then left, hurrying.

Others began to trickle into the store. It was notable that no women were on the street. Talk buzzed. Occasionally Sayre walked nervously and impatiently to the front of the store and peered out, looking uptown in the direction of the courthouse where Lou Trinidad's office was.

After about ten minutes, Trinidad came in, followed by Stanek. Sayre said, "You're the sheriff of this county, Lou, and this wild shooting in town has got to stop. Hilda Jorgensen is dead, and there may be others for all we know." The crackle of distant gunfire seemed to punctuate his words. "There's no excuse for it. Patch ought to be able to keep the peace without smashing every window on the street and killing half the citizens."

Trinidad said sourly, "Get rid of him then."

Sayre's face was questioning. "We've tried that. We've tried everything we know short of shooting him."

"Then try that, too." Trinidad's voice was cold and thin with unconcealed rage.

Sayre stared at him. He understood Trinidad's anger at Patch, but until now Sayre hadn't realized how vicious and vengeful that anger was. Others had heard Trinidad's words, and now everyone seemed to be trying to speak at once. Sayre noticed that no one spoke out against the suggestion.

The lack of opposition shocked Sayre

momentarily. He raised a hand. "Wait a minute! This is no way to talk!"

Trinidad glared at him. "You'd just better make up your mind what it is you want. You say you want to be rid of Patch. You say you want the gunfire stopped out there in the street. But you get all righteous when somebody suggests shooting him."

"There ought to be some say of doing it without breaking the law ourselves," Sayre said.

"All right. I'll form a posse so that the legality of it won't bother you." There was vengeful savagery in Trinidad.

Sayre was silent for a moment, frowning with his thoughts. As mayor, it was his job to see that the gunfire in the streets was stopped. But this . . . Trinidad had suggested a posse which wasn't going to be a proper posse at all. It was going to be a firing squad. Trinidad didn't have the courage to face Patch even with a posse at his back so he was planning the marshal's execution. There wasn't any other way of putting it.

While Sayre hesitated, Trinidad turned to the others. "How about it? How many of you are willing to serve?"

Nobody spoke. Trinidad said with harsh contempt, "Remember this, all of you. This is your town. This is where you and your families live. There's no telling who's going to get shot next. You all knew Luke Mills, and you know he wasn't a criminal. Neither was Andrew Oxley, and neither was Will. Phil Miller may not have amounted to much, but he wasn't a criminal. And Hilda was as nice a girl as ever lived. Those are the people Patch has killed – four of them today. Those are the kind of people he'll go on killing if he isn't stopped."

Sayre asked, "Exactly what have you got in mind?"

"I'll deputize every man here so there'll be no question about legality. Then half of us can get up on the roof of this place and half up on the second floor of the hotel. When Patch comes by, I'll yell at him to throw down his gun and surrender himself to me. If he doesn't do it – well, I guess we'll have to treat him just like any other criminal."

Sayre was watching the faces of the men. Hesitation had been in them at first, but Trinidad's talk of deputizing and legality seemed to have quieted their doubts.

The front door of the store opened, and Claire came in. She looked at the townsmen grouped inside the store. "Why aren't you out there helping him? Isn't this your town, too?"

Trinidad said, "What we're going to do is stop him, not help him. He's gone clear out of his mind."

She stared at the sheriff unbelievingly. "Stop him? From catching the men who killed Hilda Jorgensen?"

"From shooting up the town. There are ways to settle things without killing a lot of innocent bystanders."

"What ways? And how are you going to stop him? Just exactly what have you got in mind?"

"I'm getting a posse up, if it's any of your business. We'll call to him to surrender and throw down his gun."

"And if he won't?"

Trinidad scowled at her. "If he won't, then we'll treat him like we'd treat any dangerous criminal."

Claire shifted her look to Sayre. "Mr. Sayre, you're not going to allow this are you? This is going to be a lynching, even if the sheriff is leading it. You know it is."

"Miss Claire, this shooting has got to stop. The killing has got to stop. Hilda Jorgensen . . ."

"Frank didn't kill Hilda Jorgensen!" Claire screamed.

"But he was to blame. If he'd quit when we asked him to . . ."

Claire stared unbelieving at Sayre. "You're agreeing to all this! You're actually agreeing to it! You're the mayor and Lou Trinidad is the sheriff, and the two of you are helping to form a lynch mob! You're willing to kill Frank to get rid of him!"

"All he has to do is surrender when we call out to him."

Trinidad interrupted harshly. "We're

wasting time. Come on, about half of you. We'll go up on the roof. The rest of you go across the street to the hotel and get places in the second story windows. Sayre, open your gun case and give these men some guns."

Sayre said, "First, you swear them in."

Trinidad instructed the men to raise their right hands. He swore them in hastily. Sayre went back to the gun case and opened it. He passed out guns to all those who wanted them, rifles and shotguns as long as they lasted, revolvers afterward. Half of the men trooped toward the rear of the store where the ladder that led to the roof stood. The rest of the men crowded past Claire and went out into the street.

Claire stared after them with helpless, white-faced anger. Then, without a word, she followed.

Chapter 20

Dan Joslyn didn't remember all that had happened after Hilda Jorgensen had been shot. But he remembered Claire's coming to say that she was sorry Hilda was dead. He remembered shouting accusations at Patch and remembered Patch's slapping him for the second time today.

Dan had run, then. He'd run into the alley behind the jail, and on down to the railroad tracks, and along the railroad tracks to the bridge over Cottonwood Creek. Here, beneath the bridge on the grass beside the creek, he flung himself on the ground and sobbed hysterically, weeping as he had not wept since he was a little boy.

Hilda was dead. It must be a nightmare from which he would soon awaken. But he knew this was no dream.

He was already wide awake. Hilda's death was something he'd have to live with all the rest of his life because it was his fault. If he hadn't quarreled with her . . . if he hadn't run off to ask Patch whether it was true about Patch's marrying Claire . . .

Dan's loss, his guilt, his hatred of Patch . . . these were hurts, like physical hurts – no, worse than physical hurts because physical hurts will heal. These wounds would go on hurting, forever.

Faintly Dan heard the gunfire from the direction of the depot and the cattle pens.

He was all mixed up about Patch. He hated the marshal for his stubbornness, stubbornness that had brought on Hilda's death. He hated Patch for slapping him just because he spoke the truth. He sat up, knuckling his eyes and staring down at the scuffed and dusty boots Patch had given him.

He wanted to yank them off and throw them away, but he realized that if he did, he'd have to walk all the way back to town in his stocking feet. Besides, he didn't really want to lose the boots.

He didn't know what he wanted. That was the awful part. He just wished things could be as they were before all this trouble began about getting rid of Patch.

Dan got up and started in the direction of the town. He knew he had to go back. He couldn't hide here. He couldn't hide himself away from the things that troubled him.

The gunfire had stopped once more. But as he walked along the bottom of Cottonwood Creek, he heard the shooting start again. He heard the boom of a shotgun, twice. He heard a rifle crack. And he heard the sound of Patch's revolver again.

He stopped, listening until the gunfire had ended. Then he went on. He climbed out of the creek bottom at Texas Street and walked along the upper side of Texas to Elm Street.

Elm Street was deserted. There was not a soul in sight. Not a living soul, at least. Dan's heart stood still as he saw a body lying in the street.

But it wasn't Patch. Almost at once Dan's instincts told him that. The body was that of Phil Miller, who sometimes worked for Locke at the Alamo. Phil must have been one of those who had ambushed Patch and had killed Hilda. Locke must have been the other killer. Dan supposed Patch was pursuing Locke right now.

Dan stood on the corner of Texas and Elm streets for a long, long time. He didn't know where to go. He didn't want to go home to Ma Jorgensen's boarding-house. He didn't want to hear the awful sounds of her grief. He didn't want to answer her questions about what Hilda had been doing at the jail. Not yet. Sometime he'd have to face those questions and answer them, but not right now.

He stared uptown. His eye caught movement in the upstairs windows of the Kansas Hotel. He watched the hotel for a long time, finally seeing movement in the other windows, too. There were men

284

in all the front windows of the hotel, he realized suddenly, in all six of them. They had the windows open, and they were waiting for Patch to appear so that they could shoot him down.

Now Dan stared at the other buildings lining Elm, one by one. He saw nothing unusual in any of them until his look rested finally on Sayre's Dry Goods Store. There he saw men on the roof, barely visible, showing only the tops of their heads as they peered over the parapet. He counted four heads, but he realized there might be more.

Another ambush had been laid for Patch, but this time the marshal would not escape. This was an ambush he could not escape.

Dan had to find Patch and warn him! He had to find Patch right away! If he didn't find Patch, the marshal would be killed.

Dan started to run but now he stopped. He stopped and stood there uncertainly, thinking of Luke Mills, of Andrew Oxley and of Will. Not one of the three had been a criminal, yet now all were dead by Patch's gun.

Up there in the hotel . . . and there on the roof of Sayre's Dry Goods Store . . . those men weren't criminals any more than Mills or Oxley or Will had been. Yet how many of those men on the roof would die, if he told Patch that they were there? And if he did not tell, then Patch would die.

Dan began to shake. His body trembled as though the day were bitter cold. His teeth chattered, and he felt like throwing up. How was he going to decide who was to live and who was to die? It was too much to expect of him. But if he did nothing, then that would be a decision in itself, the decision that Patch should be the one to die.

Dan took one more look at the upstairs windows of the hotel. He took one more look at the roof of Sayre's Dry Goods Store. Maybe Patch had been stubborn and selfish in refusing to quit when they asked him to, but Patch had not been wholly responsible for the deaths today. The town must share the responsibility because it had wanted to rid itself of Patch no matter what had to be done to accomplish that end.

Dan had to warn Patch, but he had to do more than that, too. Patch was his friend. Patch was the closest thing to a father that Dan had had.

He turned and ran toward the jail. There were guns in the jail, and the door was unlocked. Maybe one gun, coming to Patch's aid, would give the marshal the time he needed to save his life. Dan could only hope so.

Patch tried to watch for every potential hiding place ahead of him, but that was not an easy thing to do. The alley was narrow, and there were sheds and fences all along its length. He hoped he could drive Locke into the open, or at least out into a street that would be wider than this narrow alleyway. Patch had a healthy respect for the shotgun Locke was carrying, knowing what it could do to a man at short range. Patch had seen men literally cut in two by a shotgun blast.

Locke was heading uptown into the residential district, and Patch didn't like that a bit. Already one bystander had been killed, a young girl at that. He didn't want any more innocent people killed, but neither did he intend to let Locke get away. Since Patch had no authority outside the town of Cottonwood Springs, he couldn't raise a posse and go after the fugitive. And Patch didn't intend to leave catching Locke to Lou Trinidad because if he did, Locke would probably get away.

Patch came out into the cross street above Texas Street and saw Locke disappear around the corner into Elm. The marshal sprinted recklessly after him, knowing very well that Locke might have stopped and turned to wait for him around the corner.

Patch rounded the corner wide, only to find that Locke had ducked through a vacant lot into the alley again.

Patch followed, still running

recklessly, following the sound of weeds broken by Locke's passage through them or the sound of an accidentally disturbed tin can or other trash.

But as Locke proceeded uptown into the heart of the residential area, it was also possible for Patch to follow him by the sound of barking dogs.

Several times Locke hid out, crouching behind a fence, lying down in some tall weeds, while he caught his breath. Twice Patch located him by the ragged, panting sound of his breathing. Always the chase went on, with Locke staying ahead of Patch, but not far enough ahead to lay in ambush for the marshal.

Half an hour passed. Patch was near exhaustion now and knew Locke must be, too. Patch kept trying to drive Locke back into the business section of town, to drive him the way he would have driven a steer, and at last Patch succeeded in getting Locke headed straight down Elm.

From doorway to doorway Locke

went, pausing in each one, whirling and poking the shotgun out, forcing Patch to stop each time he did. After catching his breath, Locke would duck out again, weaving as he ran, until he reached the safety of another doorway or building corner or passageway.

The hotel was now ahead of Locke. Here he darted into the middle of the street, obviously trying to cross for some reason known only to himself.

Patch could still see Phil Miller lying where he had fallen. The street beyond Locke was deserted. As Locke reached the middle of Elm, Patch raised his gun, sighted carefully, fired and immediately fired again.

Both shots had been aimed carefully, but Patch knew that if either missed, the spent bullet could only ricochet harmlessly down the street.

Neither bullet missed. The first shot took Locke's legs out from under him. Before he could fall, the second bullet struck him squarely in the back.

His smoking gun in hand, Patch

walked steadily and carefully toward Locke, who was writhing on the ground. Locke had dropped the shotgun as he fell, but it was still within his reach. Patch reached the gun, bent and picked it up. He checked its loads, then holstered his own revolver and turned again toward Locke.

The man was conscious. His eyes glared at Patch with helpless virulence. Patch realized Locke's spine had been shattered by the second bullet. Even if Locke lived, he would never walk again.

Patch started to turn away. He heard a shout from the direction of the jail. He swung his head to look, as a second shout came from the roof of Sayre's Dry Goods Store. The words of the first shout had been impossible to understand because of the distance. Those of the second were very plain. "Patch! Throw down your gun and put up your hands!"

For an instant he froze there, doing nothing, while his mind tried to assess the threat. He could see Dan running toward him from the jail, a rifle in his hand, shouting and pointing toward the rooftops. Patch turned his head and looked at the roof of Sayre's Dry Goods Store. Several men were standing there, men with guns.

Instantly the similarity between this situation and the earlier one in which Hilda had been killed became obvious to Patch. Dan had almost reached him now. Dan might die as Hilda had unless. . . .

There was no hesitation in Patch after that. All he could think of was preventing the men on the roof from pouring bullets into the street. He had to force them to keep down until Dan was safely under cover. Patch whirled and brought the shotgun up.

Five men fired on him almost simultaneously from the roof. Five rifles poured smoke and bullets into the street. Like an echo, four more rifles and two shotguns fired from the upstairs windows of the hotel.

Patch never even saw the men in the

windows of the hotel. He fired the shotgun reflexively, automatically, in the direction of the men on the roof of Sayre's, although he was dead before the charge left his gun. He was driven back, the smoking shotgun clattering from his grasp. Before he could fall, the other bullets and the charges from the two shotguns struck him and drove him back the other way.

Literally riddled where he stood, Patch was flung to the street like a limp rag doll. He was quiet before the broken glass that he had shattered with his shotgun had stopped tinkling onto the boardwalk in front of Sayre's.

Frank Patch was dead, and now the townsmen came down from the second story of the hotel. They came down from the roof of Sayre's Dry Goods Store. They came out of their shops and out of their homes, and they walked along Elm to where Patch lay, in subdued and frightened silence, in awe over what they had done. Patch lay on his back, staring sightlessly at the sky in which a few puffy white clouds hung motionless. The autumn sun beat warmly down into his face.

Dan reached the body first. His face was gray with shock. Tears stood in his eyes, spilling over and running across his cheeks. "You murdered him! You killed him, an' all he tried to do was catch the ones that killed Hilda!"

Claire came from the Goliad, running. Twice she fell in the dust of the street, twice she got up and came on again. She stopped when she reached Patch's side and stared down numbly at this man who had seemed so indestructible to her before. Slowly, almost reverently, she knelt at his side, as if only by kneeling could she express her deep respect. There were unshed tears in her eyes, and her face was white with shock.

Dan faced the shamefaced townsmen who were gathering in the street. His outrage was too much for him to contain. His voice broke with emotion as he lashed out at them, "There wasn't an outlaw alive that could kill him, but his friends could, couldn't they? The ones he spent his life protectin' could shoot him down like he was a dog!"

Trinidad scowled savagely, "Shut up, kid! What the hell do you know about it anyway?"

Dan knew he ought to do what the sheriff told him to. He ought to shut his mouth, but someone had to speak out for Patch, and there was no one else.

Dan's face was bloodless; his whole body, cold. He looked straight at Trinidad. "Was what he done to you worth killin' him for? You're the sheriff, an' you're supposed to uphold the law! But you led the mob!" He turned to focus on Sayre and said bitterly, "Mr. Sayre, if this is the way decent men are supposed to act, then I guess I want to be something else."

Sayre had difficulty meeting the boy's eyes. "Dan, we didn't mean . . ."

Trinidad interrupted savagely. "Don't apologize, Sayre. And for God's sake, don't lie about it. We meant to kill Patch, or we wouldn't have shot at him.

The kid's right. It was a mob. And I led it for you." Trinidad's fury was no longer directed at Dan. The sheriff had let Patch's humiliating him earlier make him ignore his lawman's oath. Could he live with himself after this? And what of these self-righteous, law-abiding citizens who had let themselves be talked into becoming part of it?

Trinidad turned away toward the courthouse at the upper end of the street. Sayre and the others stared uneasily at Dan, at Patch lying in the street, and at Claire kneeling silently at his side. Then the townsmen ducked their heads, turned and hurried guiltily away.

Patch stared at the blueness of the sky while Dan Joslyn sobbed with helpless bitterness. He had taken his stand with Patch. Dan had tried to save Patch but had failed. Dan wasn't going to be very well liked in Cottonwood Springs from now on, but he didn't care. He had said only what was true.

Frank Patch lay dead, but there was a part of Patch that would never die. It